REPURPOSED

REPURPOSED

LoRee Peery

Dedication

To all the females in my life. Family first. My sister Renee; daughters I've birthed Paige and Chantell; daughter by marriage Debbi; daughters-in-law Randi and Ana; granddaughters Loren, Hannah, Jaeden, Angelica, Olivia, and Alaina; and great-granddaughter Zaniyah. Also, my many nieces and cousins. You are who you are by the grace of God—beautiful daughters of the King.

To my countless Christian sisters whose hearts I see in their eyes and whose actions have blessed me, along with multiple others who don't look at the outside.

To Peggy Cline, whom I hadn't met until she reached out to me following one of my surgeries. Thank you beyond measure for the shining example of walking and serving a Christian life. And thank you for a special gift. You know what that is…

And to the Band of Bookie Sisters, a name given with tongue in cheek by one of our book club members, who range in age from young to life-seasoned. We share the love of Christ and love the reading experience.

Thank you all for enriching my life with your love.

Dear Reader,

Thank you so much for investing your time to read my story.

Can you identify with the self-image issues I've addressed? If you're female, I'm sure you can. I am presently overweight, and according to BMI charts, even obese. I grew up during a time when pressure to be thin was everywhere. Since I'm not very tall, short-waisted, and have a broad ribcage along with wide shoulders, I've always felt too big. (Even when I was thin, and that's a shame.) Unfortunately, I voiced my negative body image in front of my daughters. The enemy used that to impact them both, but their stories are not mine to tell.

It took a long time to recognize, based on Psalm 139, how I am fearfully and wonderfully made (unlike the round rectangle I see myself as). God knows every cell and atom of my body. If I criticize my outward appearance, I'm slamming God because I am the way He made me. If I diet and think about ways to take off pounds, I'm not focusing on the Lord. (Besides, diets don't work.) He loves me as I am, and I am one of His creations. HE DOES NOT MAKE JUNK.

My hat's off to anyone who is a youth pastor. It takes a unique personality, one with a childlike heart such as Cooper's, to lead and guide our young teens, especially the troubled ones. But like every pastor in the world, and those adults who serve with them, our church leaders are flawed people who choose to answer God's call.

If you aren't ready to leave Talia and Cooper yet, you could revisit them by writing a review. I value the time you as a reader spend reading my stories, and a few words on

Amazon can count for much.

May you find the grace to accept who you are, in whatever shape your earthsuit takes. Be kind to yourself, as a uniquely designed child of God. Place your dreams in His hands, no matter how wild. He has you covered according to His time. And He has a purpose for your life.

In Him,

LoRee

First reaction—gorgeous cover. Second reaction—ohhhh time travel. Third reaction—hmmm, not your usual time travel. This story is a delight to read, as Calissa learns about her grandparents through sparkling glimpses of the past and how that relates to the present and her relationship with Monte. A joy to read.

Have you ever pictured something and then tried to make everything be as you pictured it? Calissa keeps seeing her grandparents and dreaming of a life just like theirs. Will her dreams hinder or help her find happiness? Monte has been best friends with Calissa for as long as he can remember. He has his reasons for not taking the relationship to the next level. Will his ideas and hers ever line up? Or will they find if they let go and let GOD things will be even more amazing?

Miss Peery knows how to weave all this and more into an inspirational story you won't soon forget.

Thoughts on Repurposed

Ms. Peery has hit home with a story that really had me on my knees. Talia's story is mine and I'm still living it. The reader gets a sense of what the characters felt deep in the soul. As a reader, I felt they were right next to me. The flow, the way the topics were laid out, all came full circle and touched my heart. I can't wait to share this story with the world.

I enjoyed the story. Such a good reminder. I believe this story will help many!

About Repurposed

Talia Ashby is a perfectionistic data analyst who, on occasion, sees her "fat" self when she looks in the mirror. As a svelte former obese girl, she reunites with her secret teen crush, now a pastor in the church she attends.

Cooper Valiant is dazzled upon meeting a high school friend he doesn't immediately recognize due to her drastic weight loss. Since his sister had an eating disorder, he'd often felt empathy toward Talia as classmates teased and bullied her. In his pastorate position, he asks her to help girls in the youth group come to grips with body-image.

While working with the girls, Talia's recollections of youthful hurts stir up past insecurities. She must reassess her spiritual journey, and what bothers her in the present.

Added to the mix are her reawakened emotions toward the man who once came to her rescue. Will their joint journey include a personal relationship?

Key Verse

Ascribe to the LORD the glory due his name; worship the LORD in the splendor of his holiness.

~ Psalm 29:2

Chapter 1

"OH, NO." THE SCENT OF gasoline combined with heat from the late August sun had already turned Talia's stomach. Now a twist of despair completed the knot in her gut. "I can't believe I let this happen again."

The clunk of a nozzle sounded from the other side of the pump, followed by a footfall scrape against concrete. She ignored whoever stood behind her.

"...how could you?" Talia moaned and pressed her forehead against the top of the car window frame. Muted motors merged and gave way to the noisy buzz in her head.

Cookie leaped to the driver's seat and stuck her hairy gray paw through the crack in the window.

"Sorry, not your fault, baby. I'm an airhead."

"Hey, don't call yourself names."

Talia jerked at the masculine voice near her shoulder, mortified her folly had been witnessed. Blank space replaced the dilemma in her mind.

It took concentrated effort to keep an exclamation of recognition from escaping her lips. Cooper Valiant. Hero, and ninth grade through graduation crush. After all this time, he wore the same infectious wide grin. Flashing deep blue eyes were now accented by character revealing crow's feet. Attractive laugh lines set off his smile. He'd turned into a whole lot of endearing man.

"It can't be that bad."

"Uh. The door's locked. With my keys inside." She

shifted her attention away from his face as a loud pickup engine roared to a low rumble, and grounded herself again in the present surroundings.

"My dog did it." She sounded like a dolt. At the familiar resounding thud that signaled a full tank, she swiveled and reached for the gas nozzle hanging from her Jeep. "I guess I need help."

"Here. Let me." He notched the handle onto the tank and twisted on the gas cap.

A guy in a tricked-out pickup pulled behind her Jeep and gunned his motor. Cooper waved at the driver and signaled for the man to switch to another pump.

He revved his engine a couple times, and then backed up to park in another line.

Talia shrugged, her cheeks heating as she grabbed the receipt. "Cookie's done this before."

"Huh?"

"My golden." She wiggled her fingers through the window in the face of her adorable hairy, gray dog. Cookie's back legs bounced on the driver's seat, searching for purchase, with tongue lolling from a goofy grin.

"Your golden what? Never seen one like it. Still a pup?"

"Yes. Nine months. A high energy goldendoodle. The poodle is obvious by the hair. She's smart and obedient like a golden retriever, so she makes a great companion. And she cheers me up just because she doesn't have a care in the world other than keeping me company."

"She looks happy. I'd be happy, too, in the presence of such a beautiful woman." He paused and sobered as if he'd spoken without thought. "I won't apologize but that was out of place. As for your dog, I'd love to hear more about her. But it seems her energy has put you in a pickle. Will I be okay if I try to get my arm through the window?"

"Sure. She's a lovable marshmallow, safer than a cat. But my keys are further away than your arm can reach."

He rounded the hood, shot her a challenging just-watch-me grin over the top as his hand disappeared inside the passenger window. Much to her surprise, the lock clicked open.

Talia refrained from making a face at him. He'd hit the button on the door to release the handle rather than reach for the keys on the seat, where she would have sought the fob with her shorter arm. Guys just plain thought different than women.

As she grabbed her receipt, their gazes met again, and connected in a way that erased mature thought from her head.

"We're holding up the line." He flashed that ever-ready smile. "Nice ride, by the way. Purple suits you. I suggest you find another place to sling your keys the next time you get gas."

He'd always been one with a ready answer.

Cookie slapped her front legs over Talia's arm, so she body blocked the dog from escaping as she scooped up the keys dangling from Cooper's hand. "I've got my hands full with this one. Thanks again."

How could she have forgotten the kind expression in his bright blue eyes and the thickness of heart-shaped lips that any woman would covet? Close-fitting jeans revealed that he'd kept his lanky frame, and muscular definition told her he worked on keeping in shape.

She watched him climb into a sporty yellow two-seater. Cooper was dressed in a salmon Tee shirt, perfect for the fall season, not quite his favorite shade of orange, if she remembered right.

Why run into him again now? Just at the time she was taking on a new way of serving. She forcibly pulled herself together, took two deep breaths, and then engaged her own car ignition.

Talia broke into a satisfied grin. He hadn't recognized her. Wouldn't he have been surprised to know she was the fat girl he'd befriended back in high school?

✝✝✝

Fifteen minutes later, Cooper was still dazzled by the breathtaking woman at the gas station. God had to have had a hand in his safe arrival at Southside Fellowship. He sure hadn't paid attention to driving. She was beyond beautiful and svelte at three inches shorter than his six feet, shapely, feminine, and physically fit. Yep, he'd checked out her fabulous, toned long legs.

His mind still on the stranger's exotic appearance, captivated by her wide-spaced brown eyes and jet-black hair, he checked his thoughts and said a quick prayer to get into the groove of youth pastor. He climbed out of his sports car and raced across the lot.

Upon entering the church, he paused to gaze at the banner above the chest-high welcome counter. All who entered the church building were greeted with the statement on the sign: GOD'S LOVE MAKES ALL THE DIFFERENCE IN THE WORLD.

"Hey, how ya doin' tonight, Pastor Cooper?" June Rose, Pastor Kendall Winston's wife, greeted him from behind the counter. "Are you all ready for Fall Explosion?"

"I keep reminding you that it's plain Cooper. I'm as ready as I'll ever be. This place was too quiet over summer." He cocked his head at the pint-sized woman with short white hair. "Don't you take a break from being his secretary and receptionist?"

She patted her hair and smiled wide. "Service for the Lord, Cooper, isn't work. Besides, I've always believed the senior pastor's wife needs visibility."

"Bless you for standing by him. I hope to have a helpmate one day. But I doubt the Lord's plan for me is in the pulpit. Better get inside."

He entered the designated classroom and found a seat in the front row. His mind still filled with images of the classy gal back at the station, he paid no attention to the chatter as volunteers took seats behind them. Before long, Pastor Kendall stood and welcomed them all, albeit standing stiff except for his white-toothed smile. "I don't know about you, but June Rose and I are especially pumped to get this new fall off to a great start. We'll begin with the ministry leaders telling us who you are, followed by the rest of you."

Cooper zoned out through introductions of other group leaders from tots up until he heard his name announced for junior high. He raised somewhat out of his seat and waved without making eye contact, and then nudged the high school pastor to stand up and take his turn. Starting with preschoolers, all kids except the high schoolers got together on Sunday nights, met on Wednesdays during choir rehearsal and mid-week Bible school for adults. He perked up at Pastor Kendall's voice, tuned back in.

"I'm glad to welcome a couple of you who are new to Southside Fellowship. We'll start in the back. Please tell us how you came here and a little bit more about yourselves. Then we can all get to know one another."

Cooper always got a kick out of the senior pastor's thick

blond curls, perpetually untamed at the nape, and an easy object for distraction, same as the kid he was at heart. In contrast to Kendall's military stance, Cooper was in constant jittery motion. Even at his advanced age of thirty-one, he continued with toe tapping, fidgeting, rapping fingers on his knee, or bouncing one leg. He'd never been able to sit still. Pa hadn't believed in medication for hyperactivity. Cooper had driven certain teachers and church leaders out of their minds over the years. Figured that'd continue until the day he died, in perpetual motion.

He listened to the members as they said howdy and specified which area of ministry they'd be serving.

"Hi. I'm Talia Ashby. During the day, I'm a data analysist at a nearby hospital. I'm new here at Southside and will be working with the junior high youth."

Say what? The Talia he'd gone to school with?

Cooper's crossed knee dropped to the floor as he swung around. He scanned the chairs behind him, seeking the girl he'd known in school. He noted the woman who stood. Who wouldn't? She turned and he caught her face from the front rather than profile. *No way*. Talia was the beauty from the gas station? He would have fallen over, had he been standing.

Someone said, "Glad to have you."

"Because of my own rough younger years, I believe God wants me to befriend teen girls. So that's why I'm here." She flashed that gorgeous smile that hit him in the solar plexus. "Actually, I knew Cooper from when we were in school."

His mouth dropped open in shocked disbelief. This stunning woman couldn't be the same girl he once knew. She was dressed in slim-fitting mid-calf pants and black shirt trimmed in bright pink, and looked nothing like the chubby...*Sorry, Lord.* He gave himself a mental shake.

"I was rather lost in the huge congregation down the street, though I grew up going to worship there. I'd heard about Southside Fellowship from someone at work, so I visited a couple times over the summer and decided I'd like to switch memberships." She slanted a quick glance Cooper's direction, and then roamed the room. "I had quite the issues as a teen and during devotions over the summer, God spoke to me. I'm convinced His desire for me is to be a friend to young girls. The world was a difficult place for me, and I believe it's worsened. Sorry. I'm repeating myself."

"Welcome, Talia. No problem saying it twice. Your conviction comes out in your voice so that's a good thing. You can turn around now, Cooper." The group chuckled over Kendall's teasing tone. "We can all agree with his high energy, he's the perfect junior high leader and I'm sure he's glad to have you. Okay, let's continue down the row. Refreshments ahead once we hear from you remaining few."

Cooper couldn't move a muscle. How to wrap his head around this Talia Ashby compared to the heavy girl he once knew? Her creamy, coffee-tinted complexion had been clear even as a teen. Without the full face of the past, she was a knock-out with defined feminine bone structure that showed off her high cheekbones and large, almond-colored eyes. If he stared any longer, she'd think he'd turned into a stalker.

In school, he'd always gone to her defense if he heard anything derogatory, same as he went to anyone's defense if they needed it. But he'd had a soft spot for Talia and often wondered what future she'd walked into.

The unbelievable change in body size rocked him. She must have dropped close to a hundred pounds. How had it come about? He whispered a silent prayer in the hopes she hadn't endangered her health. He couldn't wait to discover the whole story.

And, Lord, don't let me get all mixed up in my thoughts, reliving regrets over Analise's eating disorder. My sister's life and Talia's are totally different.

Chapter 2

THE FIRST WEDNESDAY NIGHT IN September blew in with driving rain, which meant there'd be no outdoor activities that evening. The first person Cooper paid attention to was Talia, who sat at the far end of the front row of seats. Emotionally, she'd awakened the past. The injustice of the years she'd been bullied. Worse yet, meeting her again had triggered memories of his sister's struggle with anorexia. On some level it made no sense because Talia was far from extreme thinness. He had a hard time juxtaposing the present woman with the large girl he'd known as a teen.

He balanced one foot on the seat of a chair, hands beating a silent rhythm on his leg, and counted the youth as they entered. Cooper bounded to both feet one minute until seven. "Hey, all. Would someone please close the door? Welcome. In case you don't already know, my name is Cooper Valiant. This is Miss Talia Ashby, new to our fellowship, so give her a hand."

A spattering of claps sounded.

"Okay, find a seat, please."

The expected groans, shuffles, and lethargy went through the group.

"Our first night calls for what's known as an icebreaker so we can get to know one another. No games. Yet, anyway. As you introduce yourselves, I'd like you to share how you got your names and what they mean. You know, in biblical times, children weren't named until after an aspect of their personalities showed up, or they exhibited a God-given talent. If you haven't an answer, go ahead and use your phones to look up the name definitions. Come see me if you don't have a phone, ask a neighbor, or Miss Talia can help too."

She waved her phone in the air. Something shifted inside, shaking him up like a can of fizzing pop every time their gazes connected. Had he almost winked at her? He'd caught himself just in time.

While the teens engaged their phones, he couldn't stall his mind from going back to his own teen years. Talia had been tormented by their classmates, unless they needed her help. But she sure was smart. She always got the job done to the best of her ability, thus through school she took on leadership roles. Only in small groups. She never stood in front of the whole class except for assignments, which brought on fat jokes and belittling remarks by fellow students. As a tutor, she excelled in writing and helped other students with answers, though he often caught them taunting her behind her back.

"I'll start." He flapped his hands against his sides. "My mother chose my name because Cooper was her maiden name. I've researched it and it means an occupation. Back in the early days of English it was common to choose a surname that indicated what you did for work. Sons followed their fathers' professions. A cooper built wooden kegs to hold liquid. I'm thankful back in the day my ancestors didn't have a tavern or clean fish. Suds or catgut wouldn't fly with me."

True to form, the kids laughed.

"Just so you know, I won't stand for any mimicking or

mistreating others. Especially when it comes to names. After all, one of us could be called Booger or Bubba."

He waited for the shuffles and comments to end, and then held up a hand for silence. "The name Cooper goes all the way back to the twelfth century and refers to a maker and repairer of wooden vessels such as barrels, tubs, buckets, casks, and vats. It's also one of the oldest surnames in existence. And guess what? I'm into carpentry. My hobby is making birdhouses. Your turn now, and that includes you, Talia. Have fun, everyone."

She swiveled her chair around and encouraged the girls to form a circle with their chairs.

"Good idea there. I knew you'd be a terrific help this year, Ms. Ashby. Everyone, turn your chairs into two circles, guys and girls."

Low mumbles grew quiet except for the clicking of keypads on phones. He tuned in for Talia's voice.

"Since you each have a phone, and I already know about my first name, I'll see what I can find out about the name Valiant." She slid him a smug smile.

"Isn't that like a hero or a strong person?"

"You're right, Dustin." Talia gave him a nod. "Now I'm reading brave, courageous, and bold." She raised her head and met Cooper's gaze. "Fitting."

He saluted and turned his attention to the boys grouped around him. He jounced his knee and only gave them ten minutes, their attention spans no longer than his. Cooper leapt to his feet, clanking the metal chair against Mark's next to him. He motioned to Talia with a bow. "Let's start with you, fair lady."

She responded with a look he failed to interpret, scanned the youth from left to right as they swiveled to face the front, and then glanced at her phone. "It says my name is a girl's name. I wonder why it reads that way. Anyhow, it's of Hebrew origin that means 'gentle dew from heaven near the water.' I found that interesting. As if it only pertains to dew by water. Or dew comes from somewhere besides heaven. I like to think God chose that name for me as I walk through dew-kissed grass in the morning." She smiled and made eye contact. "Girls, let's share with the group. Who wants to go first?"

Lydia gathered her black hair in one hand, tossed it over a shoulder, and then raised her hand. "Lydia is of Greek origin, from the Bible. I've read it before, in Acts sixteen. Lydia used indigo to dye and sell purple cloths. She believed in God. It also means kind, kindred spirit."

Janiyah was the only girl in the room with close-cropped hair, but the tight kinks accented her high forehead and large eyes that balanced the symmetry of her features. "I saw a bad word in the description I won't repeat, but I like that my name means God is gracious. It's an African American name. Duh. I'm obviously that. It also says the name means I'm a terrific best friend."

"Sasha is a Russian name." She blew her light brown hair away from her mouth. "But in Greek, or the Bible, it says a form of Alexandra and means helper of mankind. Sic that what we've heard so far talks about God."

Using sic instead of cool, would he ever get used to it? Dope either, for that matter. Cooper renewed his attention on Aleah, who was the only blonde girl in the room, as she smoothed her long hair to the front over both shoulders.

"I was named after my grandmas, Ann and Leah. The computer says Aleah is an Americanized spelling of Aliyah from Arabia that means 'sublime or exalted.' In Hebrew, that's in the Bible, 'aliyah' means to go up toward God, or 'to rise, ascend.' Another biblical name."

The remaining girls were called upon before they'd speak up.

"Great job." Cooper shifted in his seat. "Guys, we're outnumbered here, but let's be strong. Who's up first?"

Mark was the shortest boy in the room. He tossed his head to flip long hair off his forehead. "Everybody knows that Mark was one of Jesus' disciples and it's a book in the Gospels of the Bible. My whole family have names from the Bible."

"Good intro," Cooper encouraged. "What does it mean?"

"Oh, my bad." Mark checked his phone. "Old Latin. In Roman 'consecrated to the god Mars.' Don't like that, but I'll take warlike in case I'm called to serve my country."

"All right. Next?"

"Gotcha. My name Dustin originated from an English surname, like Pastor Cooper's and comes from a Norman personal name." He looked down and swiped his phone. "It's probably derived from the Old Norse, and a couple names I can't pronounce. But the computer said something about Thor—isn't that like a Greek god? And stone. From old Germanic languages, it also means fighter."

Ransom spoke up without being prompted. "I was bullied in elementary school because ransom means money that a kidnapper asks for. I went home and asked my mom why I was named such an awful name. She showed me in the Bible that my name equals grace. That Jesus died on the cross as a ransom for many."

Janiyah hopped up and stretched over her chair back to give him a high-five. She plopped down like a jack-in-the-box in reverse.

"Yeah, yeah," Ransom flushed red. "Let me finish. Says my name is from England and means shield's son. I wondered if shield means fighter, kinda like Dustin's name."

"My dad told me he just liked the name Burke." The beanpole of a tall blond kid sat up straight. "It comes from a lot of places in Europe. Irish, Anglo-Norman, I don't know what that means. Habitational, guess that means a home, in Suffolk, England. Old English something that fortifies, so that must be like a fort in the old West or a castle in early Europe. It also said any of eight farms in southeastern Norway, named with Old Norse birch wood."

Mark groaned. "I didn't figure we'd have to have lessons on Wednesday night same as Sunday."

Cooper let it pass and gave the group a minute to settle into their seats and drew their attention. "This wasn't a lesson, it's a way to find out more about yourselves and one another."

"My dad says life is full of lessons."

"He's so right, Aleah." Cooper shifted his weight from one foot to the other. "By the way, make sure Talia and I have your phone numbers. I'll create a group text concerning all youth activities. I may not always sign my name, but I'll use GLMATD in texts to you all."

"What's that mean?" came a boy's deep voice from the back.

"It's based on the banner at the front entrance of the building. GOD'S LOVE MAKES ALL THE DIFFERENCE IN THE WORLD. Memorize it, since it'll be a reminder that you're never alone. You never have to face crap alone. God's got it. And He's got you."

"I wish I'd had that knowledge to cling to at your age," Talia inserted.

Cooper smiled at her and noted the time on the wall clock. "Good first time together tonight. You have two minutes to get to the gym, where we'll play a quick game. Talia, would you please help me with the cookies?" It seemed they were out the door and in the gym inside forty-five seconds. "Guys, I need two of you to put chairs side by side in the center. Then I'd like two girls to come forward, one sitting and one behind the chair." Ransom and Lydia sat.

Talia led two others to stand behind. "I have containers of sandwich cookies here. You two in the chairs, sit with your heads leaned back. When I blow my whistle, the ones behind place a cookie on their foreheads. Whoever wiggles it into his or her mouth first wins the round."

Hilarious girlish laughter and raucous boy noises filled the room.

Talia followed Cooper's example and lined the girls up so each had a turn. Often, the boys' cookies hit the floor. The girls seemed more patient and most likely won the prize. Clean-up was just as boisterous.

Before long, Talia remained the only one in the room with Cooper.

"Is it okay to say such a word in front of the kids?"

Stumped, he studied her face, but read no answer. "What word?"

"Crap. I don't like it." Her beautiful mouth turned down at one corner.

"I'll save it for the boys then. You can use flowery words with the girls."

"Life isn't real flowery, especially at their ages." She

hung her head. "I'm sounding like a prissy stuffed shirt. Or is it only guys who have stuffed shirts?"

They broke into laughter that erased the sudden tension between them.

He sobered and gave her a one-arm shoulder hug.

He remembered well the way she'd been mistreated at the junior-high level. He'd do everything he could to make her comfortable around him.

✝✝✝

Talia's mind raced as she drove home. How long would it take before she became comfortable alone with Cooper? Being around him raised the old demons of what she'd gone through as a heavy girl he'd once known. She strived to put the Lord's work into practice by spending time with the kids on Wednesdays, but the memories threatened to resurrect self-loathing emotions and raised her old sense of inadequacy.

She set her wipers on high. Hadn't Nebraska had enough rain this year? The better question, how had she ended up in the same church as Cooper Valiant, let alone working closely with him and the junior highers? "Lord, I sure hope You know what's going on here."

The past had been rolling over her since she ran into Cooper at the gas station. Would she ever overcome believing she still fell short? She knew better in her head. But hey, females were emotional. God created them that way.

She hadn't been able to fix herself as a girl so she'd determined to challenge the world around her by being as smart as she could, and sought the best grades attainable. Plus, she buried the fact she'd never, ever, had a boyfriend.

As a girl she believed everyone had seen her as a blob because most people overlooked her. No one saw her for who she was on the inside. Not Mom, Ebonee either. Nope. Mom surely hadn't meant to put her down by comparing her to her older sister. And Ebonee, as in gorgeous, slender, popular Ebonee, had always gone on her selfish way, never including her little sister.

"Stop going down that path, woman. Get those hidden emotions out of the back closet of your head and free yourself of the past." Talia hit the garage door remote, pulled in, and parked. As soon as she cut the motor, she heard Cookie hit the utility door with her paws. Thankful once more that goldendoodles didn't bark, Talia smiled all the way to the inside door. She braced herself on the landing as the pup's forelegs settled around her waist.

"I love you and missed you, too, sweetness. Now, let's dance backward so I can get inside." Who needed boyfriend hugs as long as she had this sixty-pound gangly body of fluff to love on her?

Talia knew what lay ahead. She'd be in close contact with Cooper, not only with the kids on Wednesday nights, but with him in planning the events. Maybe he was already prepared. Surely that wouldn't involve her input with lesson plans? Whatever. Now she sounded like a disgruntled teenager.

She'd need superjoined human strength when so close to him and ignore the way she'd crushed on him as a girl. All those times he'd come to her defense when others had belittled her. He was her hero turned man of God. Every moral, fun-loving, protective vein in his body would bother her on Wednesday nights from September until May.

Unless she set herself up for more torture and went to

summer camp with them all.

Chapter 3

TALIA PREPARED FOR THEIR SECOND week of youth group, excited about the blank journals she'd purchased for each girl, without Cooper consulting her over an agenda. She'd try with all her might to be a good guide, in hopes the young girls would never face what she had dealt with as a teen. Healthy in mind, spirit, and body. "Lord, give me the words I need to encourage them. Flow through me with Your words, not mine."

With the girls' wellbeing in mind, Talia considered the Bible verse on the cover of each journal, addressed a personal note to the individual girls, and wrote in the journals one after the other. Mental images of each young girl helped as the pen flowed across the opening blank page.

I pray that you will always love who you are, and who you are becoming. I pray that you have the courage and strength to unapologetically chase the dreams that our Lord places in your heart. Be a light, show the fire of your soul. Be confident, for you are fearfully and wonderfully made. Be the friend I needed when I was your age.

Be finished with established patterns that lead you to beat up on yourself. You are chosen of God. He loves you no matter what. I Corinthians 15:58 says to stand firm. Let nothing move you. Always give yourself fully to the work of the Lord.

Cookie had kept her company while she wrote with either her chin resting on Talia's thigh, or a large paw curled around her ankle.

"All right, girl. I'm finished. Let's go out and play!" She grabbed a disc-shaped throw toy and a knotted chew rope.

Cookie met her at the patio door and they had a sweaty romp in the humid evening air cocooned within the high boarded privacy fence. Back inside, Talia downed a glass of water while Cookie lapped her water dish dry.

To the cadence of the pup's panting, Talia closed her eyes. Cooper immediately filled the vision of her mind's eye. They'd spoken a brief greeting as they passed in the hallway outside the sanctuary during and after Sunday's church service, but she'd kept walking each time.

✞✞✞

Cooper finished with Wednesday's short lesson and took off with the boys.

Talia shut the door and waited for the girls to take their seats. "Hi, everyone. I'm pleased to see that you all came back for week two. I'd also like you to know that no one talked me into spending time with you or in any way forced me to spend my Wednesday nights with you. I was a teenager once, and I had a rough time of it for years. Some night soon I'll be sharing my story with you."

One of the girls made a guttural noise, but Talia couldn't see where it came from. "Okay, I don't want to bore you, but at some point I'd like to tell you the story of how God got my attention. For now, I'd like you to know that no matter how alone you might feel at times, you are never by yourself. God created each of us to have a relationship with Him."

Aleah kicked the back of the seat in front of her, drawing all eyes. "What? I don't buy it. I'm like a zit. I keep getting pinched."

A gasp followed. Then a couple chuckles. Chair squeaks.

"All right. Gather round. Soon I won't have to use the word circle." Talia swung around her own chair in front of Aleah and faced her. "Since God made us, we insult Him if we bash ourselves. I've done it myself."

She addressed the others. "Does anyone have a suggestion as to how we can change that?"

No one spoke up, but the silence told her they might make an effort to listen.

"I was a lot older than you when this exercise was pointed out to me. Try it before you go to sleep tonight. Stare at yourself in the mirror. Not to wish your hair curly if it's straight or straight if it's curly. Not to think your nose is too big or your ears stick out. Look into your own eyes and search for the positive."

She lifted the tote from the floor onto an empty chair. "Begin by talking to yourself like this. Dear Talia—say your name as I just said mine out loud—This is God. I made you. Talia, you are fearfully and wonderfully made."

Janiyah frowned. "Isn't that like being prideful?"

"Not if you bring God into the conversation."

"Do we have to say it out loud to the mirror?" Aleah flipped her blonde hair.

"If that truly makes you uncomfortable, you could write it instead. But note your features and their functions, rather than how you perceive them in a negative way. I have a journal for each of you." She pulled the first blank book from the tote and made eye contact with each girl. She had their attention, except two of the eight had dropped their chins and stared at their hands.

Talia stood, opened the inside cover to see who she'd addressed it to, Sasha, and passed it to her. She handed out the remaining blank books, and continued. "The next morning, write or say, 'Dear Abba Father,' or whatever name you choose to call our Creator God. He doesn't mind Daddy or some of the Old Testament titles such as El Shaddai or Adonai."

"What do those words mean?"

"They're Hebrew names. El Shaddai means High and Exalted. Adonai means Lord, Master. That'd be a good exercise for you to look up, the Hebrew names of God. I admit I'm not good at including those titles in my prayers. Anyway, back to what you can say to the Lord. Something as simple as 'Thank You for waking me up today' can go a long way in making your day a joyful one rather than a glum one."

Sasha sniffed.

Janiyah smiled.

Lydia wiped her cheek.

"Bring that phrase or a similar one, to mind throughout your day. And come next Wednesday night ready to share how it went. I can tell by the noise from the hall that the boys are finished with their session. Let's go work up an appetite."

✝✝✝

Cooper had been distracted all night long. Some great leader he was, aware of Talia's every movement in the same room, close to every breath she'd taken. He'd catch her eye periodically, and his mind blanked.

She hadn't made herself available as more than an acquaintance or old friend from school by her willingness to help with the youth. Cooper was hooked right away on getting closer to her. She'd drawn him in as no woman in his life before her had done. She cared for others in a genuine way that showed through her interactions with the girls. He'd have to guard his attention or one of the more mature boys would notice his spaciness.

Tonight's game was more subdued and one where the boys excelled. Two empty juice glasses waited on a table. The youth took turns flipping two keys from the edge of the table into a glass. An airborne key thumped against Cooper's thigh and pulled him out of his thoughts. He swung around and headbutted Talia, who had leaned over to also pick it up. "Ouch."

"Ugh. You're hard-headed."

Laughter surrounded them. He paid no mind. The pupils of her eyes shined with light rather than appearing black. This close to her, his breathing accelerated with how dazzling she was to gaze upon. He drew in her scent, which was alluring to his sense of smell. He was in big trouble here.

They eased to upright positions, gazes still locked.

A nudge by a sharp elbow woke Cooper from his trance. He blinked and surveyed the room. "All righty, gang, let's get this mess cleaned up. No cookies until the tables and floor are as clean as when we entered."

"Quit fighting over that dumb key." Mark grinned like a goof and reached for the only remaining chair left in the center of the room. He swung it high over his head and set it at the end of a stack against the wall. "Save your head. Don't fight over anything else you find on the floor. See ya Sunday, preach."

"Guess that leaves nothing but cookie crumbs and

napkins in the kitchen window." Talia cleared her throat and turned to walk away. The sweet citrus scent of her hair lingered following the swish of her ponytail.

"Wait." He raised an arm to touch her, let it drop. "Can we talk a bit, or do you need to take off?"

She swiped crumbs with a napkin, wiped down the counter, closed the pass-through window to the gym, and shut off the kitchen light. Finally, she gave him her attention. "I have a few minutes, walk me to my Jeep?"

He grinned all the way outside, touched her elbow, and pointed to a bench.

She took a seat in the corner, folded one leg, and set back against the iron armrest. "Do you need help with games or lessons, or something?"

He cleared his throat, jiggled his heels up and down. "I've asked the boys to come up with game suggestions, but in a pinch, there's the Internet. You and I should be open with one another, especially if one of the girls is in trouble, so we can both be available. And…" He scratched the back of his neck, scraped his top lip with his teeth. "I'd really like to know how you lost all your weight."

She gasped.

"Sorry. I know it's downright rude to bring up the subject, but I'm feeling like a mixed-up hormonal kid. I mean, have you looked in the mirror lately? You're striking. I can't juxtapose the woman you are now with the girl I knew before."

"The fat one."

"Don't use that word, please. My sister, I don't think you ever knew Analise, was four years older, and claimed to see herself in the mirror as a heavy college student when she was the extreme opposite. Anyway, she had an eating disorder. Her issues bothered the whole family. We couldn't help her. I'm just wondering about your story. Maybe it'll make me a better youth pastor so I can understand someone else with issues if I'm needed."

"No, I didn't know Analise. You mean she was like me, heavy? Or too thin?"

"Anorexic." He swiped his face. "Yeah. So, can you talk to me, please? She starved herself."

Talia drew a deep breath, exhaled, and then set a hand on his knee. "Can you hold yourself still while I gather my thoughts?"

He jumped to his feet, folded his hands behind his back, and tried to focus on a swaying tree branch across the parking lot. She breathed in two deep ones, and the buzzing in his head quieted. "That's better. Shoot."

"As for me, I thought I was living free, but I was a slave to the obsession of food to solve all my hurts. I felt guilty because I knew I wasn't taking care of the body God lives in. Knowing Jesus lived in me, and the times you stood up for me, are the only things that got me through school." She stood and faced him in the waning light. "Thank you again, Cooper."

Unable to sit still, he fingered a lock of silky hair freed of its band, and hooked it behind her ear. The world faded away. He couldn't not touch her, so he dropped his arm and sought her hand.

She stared at their joined hands, and her breathing came faster. "Thanks. That'll make it easier to talk. I wanted friends in college, longed for a different experience than I'd had in high school. Rather than turn to food, I hit the books. Eventually I bought a scale, recorded what I ate, ran in the evenings before I studied, and the pounds fell off."

"Was it hard?"

"No. It's the first time I had control of my life. I won't get into what it had been like at home. Anyway, I went down ten sizes in eighteen months. I took on more tutoring in college to pay for my new clothes. I thought I was living free for the first time, but I soon turned into a slave of food, exercise, and my scale. I mistakenly thought I was being a good steward b-y taking care of my body that God made. But He didn't have control because I didn't pray about the way I was living obsessed with every block I ran and every bite I chewed."

He couldn't help himself, he pulled her in for a hug. She fit just right against the hollow of his neck, as if that's where she belonged. He smoothed a hand down her hair. Was that lemon he smelled? "If we are truly walking with the Lord, He directs our decisions because we seek him first."

"I know that now. That's why I want to help girls any way I can."

"We'll do it together. I'm so glad we've reconnected, Talia." Though he was attracted to the point of lacking self-control, he gave himself a mental shake. The Lord wouldn't have them working closely together unless He had ordained it.

She swung their clasped hands. "I'm glad we have the common goal of incorporating the Lord into the lives of these teens, and I'm convinced I'll grow spiritually myself."

"I only wish there had been someone to help my sister. I think Analise is one of the reasons I want to help youth. I can't help feeling guilty that I ignored her. She'd always have an answer if anyone in the family said something about her not eating or the baggy sweatshirts she wore. She complained of the cold."

"Understood. I also understand your feeling of responsibility. But you were younger. No one could hold you at fault for not recognizing what was going on with her."

"Yeah. But that's in the past. Now I'm concerned about some of those kids' family backgrounds. I want you to call me out if I care too much, or butt in where you'd work best. I might even have some anxiety over the girls. A couple come from rough places and I don't want to control your methods of working with them, especially on matters of body image or bullying."

"It's dark now, and I need to get home to take out Cookie. I can't imagine you as anxious, but if you catch yourself getting rattled, give it to the Lord. And ask me to pray about it with you. He called us to serve. He'll enable us."

He gave her another quick hug, tempted beyond temptation to pull her close and kiss her. In the church lot? He released her abruptly. "Maybe you should be the youth pastor. Let me walk you to your car."

Could he be fired for carrying on this way if one of the elders saw them?

Chapter 4

TALIA SAT AT HER DINING table poised with pen above a blank page of her personal journal. Why had she waited until the last minute to do this, when the youth group met in a little over an hour? Her eyes dropped to half-mast and the pen slid from her fingers, jerking her upright.

She couldn't expect the girls to write, or view themselves differently by recording it, without her doing the same thing. She glanced at the time on her phone. *Lord, I want to grow and keep changing according to Your will for me. I must see myself as worthy. Healthy in mind, body, and spirit.*

She jotted reasons to struggle with body image issues: *rejection, fear, unwillingness to forgive (yeah, thanks, Mom), bitterness, which all result in self-absorption.*

Would she ever be able to talk about those girlish feelings that still crept up every once in a while? What if one of the girls called her out on it, or worse, Cooper? He'd been her hero, and it touched her deeper than she ever let on. He'd always spoken up if he heard others put her down in his presence. He'd stood up for her, called her smart and the others dumb for not understanding her brain instead of focusing on her body. Though he'd meant it for the best, those memories brought back her "fat girl" angst. Yes, she sure could relate to teen girls' issues.

And if she didn't guard her heart, she'd become

infatuated with Cooper Valiant all over again.

She checked the time and slid her chair back from the table. Where had the minutes gone? "Come on, Cooks, we need to go outside. Then I'm off again."

Later at Southside Fellowship, she admired the way Cooper silenced the youth with one question. "What is love?" He gave Talia a smile she took as personal, and then addressed the kids again. "Have you ever considered what love really means?"

"You want an answer right now?" One of the boys asked from the back of the room.

"Good question. I want you to think about it first. Miss Talia and I plan to come up with some topics for the next couple months and if you have input, please text one of us, or both, with questions for discussion topics. I'm thinking we could do a study on what God says about love. But that topic alone would last until you graduate."

"What will we talk about tonight?" Ever ready to get down to business, that was Sasha.

"I'd like to know who your favorite biblical characters are." Aleah addressed Talia, who had no chance to answer.

"What if we haven't grown up spending Sundays at church and don't know the Bible like you all do?"

"Another good question. Thanks, Dustin." Cooper gave a nod and surveyed the group. "God meets us where we are and we start learning from there. I'm glad you come with friends on Wednesdays. If any of you ever need a ride on Sundays, give me a holler. As for people in the Bible, you can use your research skills and find biblical heroes. Key in Moses and see if there's truth to the rumors of his height."

"I've heard of him," Burke inserted, stretching one long leg to the side. "I like best the story of David killing the giant with a slingshot."

Cooper paced the front of the room.

Talia's gaze panned from one student to the next, pleased with those who volunteered their favorites. One of the youngest girls even liked Rahab, and understood fully what prostitute meant in biblical times. As long as some spoke up and filled the room with conversation, Cooper didn't let the quiet boys get by. He waited them out, and then called on each one by name to share with the group. True to form, a lot of well-known names were tossed around.

Lydia raised her hand. "Who do you like best, Miss Talia?"

"I honestly don't have a favorite. I find that in some way I can identify with most of the women I read about. I'm drawn to them all at different times. Tonight, I'll say Esther."

Cooper rested a foot on an empty chair in front. "We'll call that good for now. I'd like you to think about love this coming week. And remember what God says about love." He used his fingers for emphasis. "First, we're supposed to love Him with all our heart, all our soul, all our mind. I'll tell you right now, I find that a mighty difficult, tall order. I'm a sinner and I'm selfish. Which brings us to the next command, another topic we could labor over. God tells us to love our neighbor as we love ourselves."

"What if we don't love ourselves?" Janiyah challenged. "I mean, I'm trash at most things I try to do."

"Aw, Janiyah, that's a heavy topic." He dropped his foot to the floor. "Talia, could you address that?"

Her head swung round as she shot him a startled glance, but she stepped forward and faced the girl. "Have you written about that feeling in your journal, Janiyah? God gives each of us specific talents that He calls gifts once we have the Holy Spirit living in us. Maybe you could try listing adjectives for love, such as God's love is perfect."

"We can try, but bottom line? I believe describing love is beyond any list we could ever come up with." Cooper placed a hand on Talia's shoulder.

Janiyah ignored his comment, and addressed Talia. "How is love perfect?"

Lydia answered immediately, her milky coffee skin tone bright. "For God so loved the world that He gave His only begotten Son, that whoever believes in Him shall be saved."

Talia couldn't be more pleased with the girl, who according to Cooper had never known her black teen father. Her teen mother had run off to California, leaving Lydia to be raised by her aunt and uncle.

"John 3:16. Can't get more perfect than that." Cooper surveyed the room. Janiyah focused on the floor. "Any other responses to how God shows His love for us?"

No one responded. Cooper grabbed a chair. "Another group is in the gym tonight, and we might need to let the younger kids have that space in the future. So, let's stack the chairs out of the way for our game. Fellas, help me clear the center of the room, please."

The girls stood and chatted in groups of two or three, except for Janiyah, who wouldn't connect with anyone. Talia crossed to her side. "Janiyah, I'm sorry you're dealing with these feelings and thoughts tonight."

The girl nodded. And shrugged. She had yet to raise her head.

Talia stepped into her personal space, their toes almost touching. Janiyah finally met Talia's gaze.

"That's better. You have nice eyes and I like to see them when I talk to you. You have school and I have work tomorrow, but go ahead and text or call so we can talk some more. Just you and me."

Janiyah raised her chin and bobbed her head from one side to the other.

Talia gave her what she hoped was an encouraging smile. "I'll pray for you."

"All right, group." Once he had their attention, Cooper explained the points of the game as he handed two girls containers holding bouncy balls, and two boys a stack of ten plastic cups each. "Let's see how many balls land in the cups. This is how it's done."

The boys' body language danced with eagerness. Most of the girls looked on with bored expressions.

Cooper reached for a ball from one of the bowls and bounced it once in the center of the floor. "Catch it in the top cup, Ransom, and put it at the bottom of your stack of cups. I'll bounce the next ball. The one with the most balls in your stack of cups wins." He bounced a ball into the cup and handed his stash to the next kid. "One and one, two for the guys. Go, girls."

Each student had a chance to play. Since there was an odd number of girls, Talia got in on the fun. All the while, her thoughts were on Janiyah and how to get the girl to recognize God's love for her.

✝✝✝

"Have a good week," Cooper yelled as the kids noisily exited the room. "I had no idea cream-filled donuts would leave more crumbs than cookies."

"That's sugar flakes from glaze. At least we aren't

working with preschoolers who spill juice all over."

"You got that right, but sugar leaves sticky stuff behind." He pulled the trash liner out of the wastebasket and hit the light. "Can you get the door to the janitor's closet for me?"

He led her through hallways, wishing he followed her because she smelled so sweet and he probably smelled like a guy who'd just been chasing balls. He pointed out the light switches so she could shut them off as they went along. Her quiet laughter tickled him. "What?"

"I happen to know security will check everything, so why shouldn't we leave the lights on?"

"Habit. Being a good steward of resources."

"I like the way you think, Pastor Coop."

"Ah, you said that like you meant it." He reached back for her hand and held it close to his side, and inhaled. He needed to find out what citrus scent she wore that tantalized his senses. Maybe it was just her.

A few moments later, he couldn't hold back his laugh. He swayed until his shoulder bumped hers. "I hope we keep meeting like this," he joked as he held open one of the main building doors. "Would you like to go for drinks? That didn't come out right. I mean decaf, tea? I get a cherry-flavored something with ice cream that there isn't a name for. Aleah came up with it just for me."

"Hmm, sounds refreshing. What do you mean by Aleah's part in it?"

"Her mom and aunt have the South Four Java and Juice down the street. Aleah and her cousin work there. I'd like to show you the study plan I've come up with for October to December, get your opinion or if you think we should discuss anything different."

"That sounds like a good idea. Should I follow you or will you come back this way if I leave my car?"

"I'd love for you to ride in my yellow canary."

She groaned and shook her head.

He tapped his fob to unlock the door, and ran around to the passenger side. "You're used to stepping up, but we ride low in my car."

"Mmm, smells good. Nice leather." She gave him a smile that zinged the soles of his feet.

He marveled anew at her present beauty. Searching her rich brown eyes, he remembered how they'd been unremarkable in the fuller face of her youth. They captivated him now.

At the South Four, she ordered a fruit smoothie that turned lavender due to berries and laughed with him as he placed his drink request. "I'll suggest to Aleah that they name your drink PC's Concoction."

"For Pastor Cooper. I like it. I have it with espresso on Saturday, without caffeine at night." In their chosen booth, he reached for her hand. "Lord, thanks for the refreshing drinks set before us. Thank You for putting Talia in my life again. Thank You for the youth group and the church we serve. Help me be the man you've chosen me to be. Amen."

He caught her hiding a smile. "What?"

"Do you always pray before indulging in a snack?"

"Habit, I guess." His knee jostled the table leg.

She laughed as though she understood he couldn't sit still. "I'm thankful to know you again, like this."

"You mean, as a crazy man instead of a crazy teen? I gotta do something meaningful with my life."

"So, Pastor Coop, tell me about how this happened. What kind of schooling does it take for a youth minister?

Did you go to seminary? I figured you'd follow tradition and build houses for the family construction business."

"I like carpentry, started with a year's study at community college east of town. Now carpentry is a hobby. I just build birdhouses. I went to church camp as a junior counselor, and enjoy still being a kid, so thought I'd give it a shot and ended up interning here at my own church. Earned a bachelor's degree from Bible College in Omaha."

"Do you have a degree in theology then?" She raised her eyes from the straw in her cup and met his gaze.

His focus lowered to a glob of pinkish stuff in the corner of her mouth. Connected with her eyes again, and then cleared his throat as he pointed. "You have, ah, something."

She leaned forward until his finger was a whisper from touching her mouth. Talia gasped as if she realized where they were. Her eyes rounded and she looked everywhere but at him as she swiped it away. Color rose in her cheeks.

He lowered his outstretched finger and lost the desire for his creamy drink. What would those sweet lips taste like? Strawberry? Cold for sure, but he'd love to warm them up. The thought hit him with a jolt and he banged the bottom of the table with his knee again. "S, suh, sorry."

"Something sting you? Ice cream headache?"

"Nah. I just had a thought and you know me, I don't sit still easy. My mom's always telling me to chill." It was way too early to confess that he couldn't stop thinking about her.

She responded with musical laughter that reminded him of soft tinkling bells accenting a Christmas melody.

"We better get to my plans." He laid his phone on the table. "Were you finished asking me about my education?"

"No theology degree, but is yours in seminary then?"

"Well, you know I took tons of Bible classes, but my

degree is in business. For some reason, probably because I'll never grow up and hope to always love the Lord at heart the way a kid does, the criteria of the elders here determined I'm qualified to lead. One of them mentors me every week in Bible study. I'm trying to memorize Psalm eight right now."

"You're blessed. I got into the Bible by making notes while online teachers spoke. I've never been close to an older Christian woman."

"Sorry to hear that. Are you close to your mother?"

Her features froze. Then a gamut of emotions filled her expressive eyes. Hurt. Regret. Guilt. Hardness. Her hand shook as she slid her napkin and plastic cup aside.

He read her silent plea and didn't push.

Her shoulders lowered as if in relief.

He drummed his fingers on the table. "Consider this opportunity as your chance to become the mentor you lacked as a girl. I have no doubt you're God's choice of an older woman to influence these teens. Once we get to know them better, ferret out their back stories, you'll be called upon to change a life."

Chapter 5

AS THEY EXITED SOUTH FOUR Java and Juice, Cooper's mind was preoccupied with the way Talia had reacted to his plans for them to attend a one-night viewing of a faith-based movie before it released in mid-October. She liked the idea of checking it out to see if they'd recommend it to the youth. Yes, the movie would be a date. He'd all but read her mind because it was on his. Talia would correctly construe the event as a date.

"Hold it."

Her demand stopped him on a dime. He half-turned at her touch on his arm.

She dropped her hand and skidded to a halt. "I don't like walking a step behind you." She squared her feet in line with his. "Is it all right if I walk beside you? Do you ever plan on answering my question?"

Her question about his family.

He'd discovered she was uncomfortable with stretches of silence. Oh, man. Two demands. How could he want her anywhere other than at his side?

"You must need conversation as much as I need to always have a body part moving. My dad is a farmer in Kansas, and Mom is a home decorator. My brothers are as obnoxious as me and haven't grown up any more than I have. Palmer, Duane, and Rory." He swallowed. This was always hard.

"You mentioned a sister?"

He didn't want to erase the bright, curious expression on Talia's face. "One sister, yes. Analise. I have trouble talking about her, and it's another reason I want to reach the youth. My sis, oldest in the family, was anorexic. She died young, only thirty-three. She'd always been thin. I guess kids nicknamed her Twig as a girl. It still torments me the way we made up stick jokes and were monstrous enough to call her a praying mantis."

Talia didn't respond. What could she say?

Inside the car, he inserted the key but didn't engage the engine, and then dug his fingers into his left knee. When it came to Analise, words didn't come easy for him even now.

"I wish we weren't in the car. I'd love to hug you. Those blasted eating disorders hurt. In the case of Analise, they kill. With a sister so thin, why in the world did you even notice me in school? I was such a blob."

Why did Talia call herself names? He started the engine. "Don't say things like that about yourself. For some reason, I saw what's inside you. In a way, you reminded me of Mom. She was obese until ten years ago when she paid out of pocket for an intense blood work-up. Come to find out, she has a thyroid condition that was never caught. Once it was diagnosed and treated correctly, she lost weight."

"I'm so glad she's healthy now."

"Not as healthy as you. You positively glow, Talia. I can't get over the way I didn't recognize you at first. You blew me away at the gas station. You sucker-punched me that night at the ministry meeting." He reached for her hand and held it on the edge of her bucket seat until he turned into the church parking lot one-handed. "All through our time with the kids on Wednesday nights, you distract me.

You dazzle me now."

"And you have a way with words, Pastor Coop." Her giggle chased a racing thrill up his spine. "I like the shortened version of your name that our girls coined for you. At their age kids can be so mean. But you never were. In fact, I thought of you as my hero." She sputtered. "Did I really just say that?"

He raised her hand to his lips and grazed her knuckles with his mouth. "We're all fearfully and wonderfully made, dear Talia. I think you're the perfect choice of woman to disciple young girls, especially those who have body image issues. I need your help. The church needs you."

"Thank you. I can't tell you how sorry I am that your sister didn't find the help she deserved."

"We all tried to help her. I have to believe she's in heaven. Before we say good night, would you go somewhere with me next weekend?"

"Somewhere?"

"Yeah. Do you like football?"

"Is one of our boys playing?"

"Not high school. The Huskers play at home a week from Saturday."

"Man, I haven't seen Big Red live since I was in college. I loved the excitement." She didn't answer his request.

He held her hand from his car to her Jeep. "God's got a sense of humor, don't you think? The way I didn't know who you were. Who would've ever thought we'd meet again because your dog stepped on the keys and locked the door? You're so beautiful that I felt like a teenager at that gas station."

She smiled that smile that stole his breath. "I learned my lesson. I don't toss my keys on the passenger seat any longer. Thank goodness I had the window down for Cookie that day. I knew right away, because it's happened before. I knew I couldn't reach my keys on the seat."

"I didn't even think about trying to reach them on the seat. The handle's closer."

"Men and women don't think alike." They shared a laugh. "I suppose you'll bring that up often, won't you?"

"We'll see. It's fun to hold something over you that keeps you in line."

She slapped him with the side of her purse. "You absolutely do not have to keep me in line. I'm not a teenager."

He whistled. "You don't have to remind me of that fact. Now, what about that Husker game?"

✝✝✝

The following Wednesday, Talia faced the gaggle of girls arranged in a circle and opened her Bible on her lap. "I'd like to begin our discussion by reading what Pastor Cooper just talked about. Galatians 4:7 says, 'So you are no longer a slave, but God's child; and since you are His child, God has made you also an heir.' Do any of you have questions, or need clarification on what that means, or do you need more discussion on biblical love?"

Sasha blushed and ran a hand over her open Bible page. "Once we stop messing up our lives and ask Jesus to take over, we become God's children. He forgives, and we know heaven's up ahead."

"Thank you. I couldn't have said it any better. Just imagine yourself a daughter of the King. I'd like for each of us to read the verse again silently. Figure out exactly what these words mean to you. None of us likes to think we've lived a life of sin. That basically means that once we know something we do or think is wrong and we continue to do it, that act becomes sin."

"And it bites 'cause it includes our thoughts," Lydia pointed out. "My mom says sin starts in our heads."

"You have a wise mother. Don't read the verse fast, think about each word, each promise. Then whoever would like to share, please do."

Most of the girls glanced up briefly and shifted in their seats, but didn't meet the gaze of anyone else.

Talia gave them three minutes, which judging by their expressions was an eternity for the girls. No one opened up, but their frowns and fidgets spoke volumes. They all kept their eyes lowered.

"All right, I'll bare my soul to you. I didn't grow up pretty like all of you. I was overweight my whole life. I'll never forget how shattered I was the time my mother took me shopping for new clothes. I was four years old. The sales clerk in the girls' department all but sneered at me. She had thin lips and said to my mother, 'Big girls like her have to go to the other department. She needs a size 6x.'"

Varied expressions peered back at her. She had everyone's attention.

"College was underway when I tore up my high school yearbooks. Seeing those pictures of me as head of the editorial staff, and the other clubs most kids called nerdy, made me gasp and cry. I had no idea how awful I must have appeared to others. My eyes were almost lost in chubby cheeks and puffy eyelids. I never realized how big I really was compared to the others."

"But you're classy and fit now," Aleah said.

"Thank you. It was a lot of hard work. Before that,

though, I said worse degrading things to myself, like, 'Who'd ever want you?' Then I'd bury my sorrows, my emotions, in copious amounts of food. In public, I'd slink into a room hugging the wall. Now I enter with my head held high, with thanks for the confidence the Lord gives me. I remind myself on a regular basis that He looks at the inside of a person rather than the outside."

"Isn't it better to want strength rather than worry about being overweight or too thin?"

"That's a mature observation, Aleah. I began to see myself as strong, with help from God, as I shrank from a size eighteen to eight. I let go of regret and shame and accepted God's grace."

Janiyah opened her mouth, shut it just as quick, and then noise from the boys' side of the room interrupted.

"Sounds like it's time for our game. Remember, girls, if you have trouble understanding what pastor Cooper or I talk about, or if you have anything on your minds to sort out, we're only a text or call away. Let's have fun so we can eat."

She found herself next to Janiyah as they repositioned chairs. "I'm sorry you didn't get to speak. Remember your question or comment and get ahold of me later, okay?"

✞ ✞ ✞

Talia's phone rang at 1:10 AM. The screen read Janiyah.

"Yes?"

"This is Janiyah's grandmother." Talia strained to hear the low, shaky voice. "Um, Janiyah is in the hospital after taking a lot of my pills. She wants to see you."

Talia gasped, freed her hands by holding the phone against her shoulder, and reached for her jeans hanging off the chair. "Oh, my goodness. What happened?"

"She asked me to telephone you so she can tell you herself. It was a close call."

"Which hospital?"

Talia slipped on her shoes as she listened to the answer. She tapped off the call, grabbed her keys from the purse pocket, and patted Cookie on the chin. Almost left her phone. *What happened, Lord? Please make Janiyah be all right.*

Should she call Cooper, or let him sleep? She'd see him tomorrow for that movie date that had been moved up.

"Lord, show me what to do here, this might be out of my depth." Through the open floor plan of her great room, she called out again. "Help, Lord!"

When you are weak, I am strong.

Talia texted Cooper while her garage door swished open. *I need you! Janiyah's in the ER.*

Talia hit every red light on her way. She met Cooper at the turnstile of the hospital and they entered together.

He reached for her hand. "Do you know her room number?"

She nodded and hustled to the elevator. Inside, she watched the floor numbers light up one by one. She stepped forward at the ding for the correct floor.

"Wait." Cooper knuckled a tear from each of her cheeks. "Be strong. Do you want to pray before we go in?"

"Thanks. I talked to the Lord all the way here. I think He drove for me." She tried to smile, imagined it came out more of a grimace. "Since Janiyah asked for me, could you pray while I'm in with her?"

"It'll be my privilege. I'll see if her grandmother could use a word."

Talia noted there was no one in the hall. She kissed Cooper on the cheek. "Thank you."

The room door was ajar. Talia rapped twice and called Janiyah's name as she entered. A nurse nodded from the bedside. An older woman with white curls and cheekbones that matched Janiyah's nodded through her tear-stained face. She adjusted the colorful green and blue scarf, stood, and quietly left the room without speaking.

"Honey?" The nurse touched Janiyah's hand, the one free of an IV line.

"Wassup?"

"You have a visitor."

Janiyah swiveled her head, slashed a groggy smile. "You came."

"I did."

"Sorry it's the middle of the night."

"Don't apologize. I'm glad your grandmother called me."

Janiyah moved aside a bright blue barf bag and patted the side of her bed.

Talia sat and covered Janiyah's hand with hers. "Is it all right if I pray?"

The girl nodded and closed her eyes.

"Dear Lord God, our Daddy and King all wrapped up in One. Thank You from the bottom of my heart for sparing Janiyah. I praise You for who You are and ask that You heal her heart and body until she's as good as new. Amen."

Janiyah drew a shuddery breath. "Thanks. I couldn't get that word 'slave' from the Bible verse out of my head. My people have been slaves. I know girls who've disappeared. Pretty girls that I believe have been trafficked. I know girls who are sex slaves to older men and do whatever they're asked to do. I think this world is ugly and don't know where I fit. I'm trash. Not even good at checking out of this world." She stopped talking due to her tears, wrenching Talia's heart. "But I'm sorry for what I did. It hurt my grandma and I hate that you're not home sleeping."

"I've experienced different things than you have in life, but I can identify with your hurt. It sounds like you've gone down a path that makes you older than your age." Talia spied tissues on the counter next to the sink and brought the box within Janiyah's reach. Then she waited until the girl pulled herself together. "I can't change any of that. But God can use whatever you've gone through, and He knows exactly where you are. The Lord will make you a better and stronger person for having gone through this. Do you have anything else to talk about, or something I can do for you?"

Talia waited as Janiyah blew her nose. "Just keep praying that I understand what you and Pastor Coop are trying to tell me. That I get what God wants me to see so I can hope for what's ahead in my life. I feel helpless and hopeless."

"We're neither of those things when Jesus is in our lives. And you are far from trash, Janiyah. Remember, we are made after God's own image. Just so you know, Pastor Cooper is in the waiting area talking with your grandmother and praying."

The whites of Janiyah's eyes were huge in her dark face. "He came too?"

"He did. He cares for you. He wants you to realize the way God watches over you, dear one. Our Jesus is just waiting for you to acknowledge that you need Him and longs for you to turn your life over to Him."

"That sounds too good to be true. Why would He want

me?"

"We all matter to God. He created you the same as He made everyone else. He desires for all of us to want Him in return. Pastor Cooper and I are here because you matter to us."

And I matter to Him. I need to see myself as God does. I advise the girls to see themselves as righteous. I need to see myself the same. Why is that so hard?

Chapter 6

ONCE HE RETURNED FROM THE hospital, Cooper bounced in and out of bed, wrestling with the covers. Wide awake, he eventually kicked the blankets to the foot and gave up on sleep. Dawn made it clear what a short night it had been. Maybe it was due to how small Janiyah had seemed on that hospital bed that painted his thoughts with images of Analise. What a waste. Yet he would never question God's timing as far as her short walk on earth was concerned.

He'd be totally wrecked if anything happened to Talia, who'd come to mean more to him than he could express in words. Searching back in his memory, something about her had always drawn him. Even as a teen, he'd seen her sweet spirit and concentrated on her pretty face. He finally admitted to himself that he'd tried to ignore what she looked like on the outside. But something about her attracted him. And he'd never stopped caring for her. Life without her would be empty, although it might be too soon to admit such a thing.

The day passed in a blur until she opened the door before he depressed the bell. Dark shadows circled Talia's eyes, and she must've given up on her ravaged hair. But the combination somehow enhanced her beauty. The smile she gave could light a night sky. "After what we went through with Janiyah, I sure hope I can concentrate on this film."

"About that movie. Would you mind if we just talk and

don't go? Besides, we've got the football game coming up." He reached for her hand and drew circles on her wrist with his thumb. "I didn't sleep because I was contemplating the frailty of young life. I might embarrass you by falling asleep."

"I'm thinking you read my mind. I've seen a movie trailer online and can't find anything objectionable about the synopsis."

"Good enough for me." He waited as she secured her door. "Is going to the South Four all right?"

"It should be, as long as Aleah isn't working. Don't want her overhearing anything we talk about."

"I've been going there long enough to know the girls work a split shift on Saturdays so Aleah isn't there in the evenings." He concentrated on driving, thankful Talia was also in a pensive mood.

At the strip mall she unhooked her seat belt and reached for the door handle.

He stalled her with a touch. Wanted to drown in those expressive brown eyes as their gazes met.

"Yes, Cooper?"

"I'm sorry. I just need to feel useful tonight. Would you be kind enough to let me get your car door?" Didn't she realize giving a courtesy benefitted him as much as her? "And maybe hold your hand during our friendly outing?"

"Don't you have that in reverse, Pastor Coop? It sounds to me like you want to show me kindness. But I'll indulge your gentlemanly manners." She rose her brows along with one hand as an idea obviously struck. "I think that's a talk to cover with the kids. Kindness would be a good topic for when we meet next."

"Let's hit on us tonight. I'm being a selfish man, and not

a good pastor example." He kept eye contact as he rounded the hood and gave her a hand out of the passenger side.

She unfolded like a delicate, yet strong, flower under the sun's warmth. The flash of her smile made him as dry-mouthed as a teenager. She reverted to seriousness immediately. "So did this thing with Janiyah hit you as hard as it did me?"

"You have no idea." He wanted to fold himself closed like a tulip ready for night. "I've thought of my sister for over eighteen hours."

"I'll gladly listen if you want to talk about it."

He led her to a pair of comfy leather chairs cozied in a corner, and thumped a hand on the fake tree stump purposed to support their drinks. "Be back in a jiff."

"Thanks, Cooper."

A few moments later, he set down the drinks and dangled his hands off the ends of the overstuffed chair arms. "My family always worried about Analise, figured if she didn't put on some weight we'd get a call about a heart attack, or her kidneys had stopped working. Maybe some other organ failure."

"That had to have been so hard. I imagine your mother never relaxed." Talia sipped her chai tea and he followed suit with his caffeinated drink.

"Janiyah had looked so tiny in that hospital bed, as small as I remember Analise, who told me once how constant prayer hadn't enabled her to accept her appearance. Mom said later that Analise had viewed her mirror image as a fat person's, and didn't know how to eat without imagining weight in places she couldn't live with. Even in the summer, my sister wore oversize sweatshirts that swallowed her emaciated body because her food portions were measured by the tablespoon rather than a serving spoon."

"They didn't make shirts big enough to hide my extra pounds. Sorry I said that. Go on." Talia wiped condensed moisture from the outside of her plastic cup onto her napkin.

"My parents tried therapy, Christian and secular. Analise claimed forgetfulness regarding the appointments and made other excuses not to go." Cooper released a pent-up sigh and took a long pull of his sweet cherry drink. "Anorexia didn't take my sister's life. Analise was asleep in her bed when a storm blew a sixty-foot tree onto the house she rented. The last time I saw her, she weighed ninety-seven pounds. Thank God for her Christian belief. I know I'll see her in heaven. That doesn't relieve the pain most of the time."

"How old were you?" Talia leaned forward and placed a long-fingered, warm hand on his knee. "Do you plan to tell your sister's story to the kids?"

He'd never given it a thought. "When she was in college, I was in eighth grade. I haven't talked about her to many people, so I don't know."

"I believe you should. You can identify with them because of your age when it happened. And Cooper, why are you so hard on yourself? You weren't old enough to advise her or help her get the professional guidance she needed."

"Thanks. I've never thought of that before, only felt guilty. You are wise and I'm so thankful we've met again. I think the girls could benefit from you sharing your weight loss and body image story with them. I'm glad you're healthy today. How'd you cope as a kid?"

"Other than have you come to my rescue?" Talia gave his knee a squeeze, released, and then swirled her blended tea. "Since I excelled in writing and helped other students with answers to their studies, it gave me the feeling I could fix other problems of the world."

He got a kick out of her air-quoting the word fix. "I'll bet the guys followed you around like lap dogs once they realized your inner beauty matched the outside."

"Never noticed. No boyfriends. Ever." Her shrug spoke volumes. "I still considered myself a glob of blubber. I got used to others seeing or appreciating me for what I could do for them rather than who I was."

"Even your mother?"

"Especially my mother." Talia's lips thinned and a muscle in her right arm twitched. "I'll always fall short compared to how Mom sees Princess Ebonee."

Cooper chuckled over Talia's repeated use of air quotes. "Now, I understand better where you're coming from. I imagine it's hard to be kind without remembering the past. Was there a particular event that made you change your eating habits?"

"Oh, yes. Classes had just begun at university. My yearbook arrived at the house while I was packing winter clothes. I checked the index for any mentions of me. I turned to those accolades and was shocked at the pictures of myself. It didn't matter that I led the editorial staff. I compared my size to the other girls. I knew I was big, but hadn't realized I was so huge."

"I never saw you that way."

"Thanks, Cooper, but it was past the time for change. I had no physical attributes, had never participated in sports. But I knew I had to take some action. So every chance I got, I walked. Oh, it was hard at first. My thighs rubbed together, my legs ached, and I didn't move very fast. But combined with healthy eating choices, the weight slowly slid off. I no longer had to wonder or face the anxiety over not fitting into a chair when I entered a room."

He finished his cherry concoction and removed the plastic lid to gulp the last swallow.

Talia stared off as though concentration would give her vision beyond the back wall.

He was certain she glimpsed into the past. "What do you see?"

"I'm eyeing myself after the weight loss. I was in the junior department at a store in the mall." She focused on him and smiled wide. "Imagine, not the department with exes following numbers. I'll never forget catching a reflection through a mirrored column. I thought it was someone else and said 'excuse me.'"

He laughed with her. What a delight to hear her story.

"I'm guilty of telling myself lies when I studied my image in the mirror."

"What do you mean?"

"As a heavy girl I had little self-worth except when I was doing my homework or helping someone else. Then I felt smart and had a sense of contributing to the good of self or others."

"How about after you lost the weight?"

"It was really hard not to see the truth. That I had an acceptable body. That somebody would finally notice me and not ignore me. I no longer imagined what they were thinking when they looked at me."

"Is that when you totally accepted yourself for who you are in Christ?"

"I tried hard, and it's still a process. I jotted in my journal. Things like: *Don't like your life? Want happiness?*

Then don't wait for circumstances or another person to change things. You need to decide to change your own world! Thank the Lord He gave me the determination to do just that. And I couldn't have done it without Him."

"I repeat. You need to share your testimony with the girls."

Her smile made him go all squishy in the middle. It was a wonder his eyes didn't cross while he sought to settle his equilibrium. She broke eye contact and played with her damp napkin. "I've already mentioned it. Now with Janiyah in trouble, you're probably right. I doubt her overdose of grandma's pills had anything to do with weight, but rather how taunts have affected her self-image. I hope she's there Wednesday night."

"I keep thinking about God's grace and a quote. Charles Spurgeon, I think. Something about every minute that the Christian lives between here and heaven should be accepted as a moment of grace."

"Oh, yes. We all need to embrace the amazing life we have only because of God's grace."

"Thank you for sharing with me, Talia. You turned around my grieving for Analise and reinforced the goal that we're meant to reach these kids using what you and I have gone through in our own lives."

"If they'll only listen. I don't know if I would have at their age."

✞✞✞

Cooper walked through the room, waiting for the noise to cease. If the kids acknowledged him, he said hello. They seemed extra rambunctious, maybe due to the cloudy day and sporadic rain.

All of a sudden, Burke slammed into him.

Cooper steadied the youth, surprised to realize they were close to the same height.

Ransom put the skids on his rushing body so he wouldn't ram Burke. "Time to quit trippin'."

Cooper needed a couple seconds to process the boy's statement. Tripping to this generation meant acting stupid or crazy.

Ransom's shoes squeaked against the tile "Sorry, Pastor Coop. New rides."

"Yeah." Burke backed up. "We're just messin' around."

Cooper scanned the brood of boys. "I know what it's like to do things just to be a butthead. I used to do the same kind of tricks at your age. It doesn't get you anywhere, especially if there are girls or children in the way who could get hurt. Just so you know, though, I'm not in the mood for such goings-on tonight."

"I'm chillaxin," Dustin inserted.

What was with the slang tonight? Again, Cooper mentally translated. His mom used to tell him to chill. She still did on occasion. The kid meant chilling and relaxing.

"Because of Janiyah, right?" Mark hung his head.

Unlike the boys, the girls were extra subdued.

One said, "I wonder why Janiyah isn't here tonight."

"Probably embarrassed."

Cooper didn't care for the owner's tone.

Talia jumped in. "She doesn't have to remain embarrassed. Every one of us has made poor choices, including Pastor Cooper and myself."

"I've almost pulled that stupid stunt, but didn't take it as far." Sasha's admission drew a varied reaction of facial expressions.

"A-a-wk-ward."

Cooper didn't want to know who sang awkward. That's exactly what this situation was. He spoke over their heads and didn't acknowledge any of the speakers by name. "When I was a kid I had a tendency to call myself stupid, or worse, if I messed up. I got hung up on my crooked teeth or straight hair and grumped around about it. It was really easy to get down on myself. My mom reminded me that God don't make no junk, so I had to snap out of it. I learned that it's all right to show kindness to myself."

"What if we don't have a parent who stands up for us no matter how big or little the stuff we're goin' through?" Dustin seemed so together. He had to be referring to someone else.

Then again, did any pastor know what went on in the homes of others? "As I said, I was a butt at times. We all mess up. Even our parents. No one is perfect or does the right thing all the time."

"Yeah, yeah," Random added with enthusiasm.

Talia stood by Cooper's side. "Excuse me for interrupting, but you just called yourself a name. That doesn't fly here, right? I remember how kind you were to others. There was a fat girl in class whom kids made fun of. We didn't call it bullying so much as teasing at the time. However, it was belittling." She scanned the group, meeting their gazes. "But your pastor stood up for that girl and it made a big impression. He had to feel better about himself after showing kindness to someone else."

"Kindness. The love your neighbor as yourself that Jesus talked about." Cooper took over. "Time for us to get moving tonight. Grab a seat. If any of you want to talk about what's happened with Janiyah, Miss Talia or I would be glad to meet with you privately. But that's all we'll say about it tonight. My assignment for the week is to keep your ears and eyes open for a friend, or maybe a lost soul in school, who needs a break. It could even be a neighbor on your street or a family member. I want you to do a good deed for someone who needs it. Then let us know how that turns out."

"Is that kind of like being the only Jesus someone might see?" Ransom's voice cracked with his question.

"Exactly." Cooper grabbed a chair. He didn't sit, but used it to prop up a leg and where it held his folded arms. "I like Talia's example of sitting in a circle, so gather round guys, while the girls get into their group."

✝✝✝

Talia began talking right away. "Remember what we discussed last week? A couple of you weren't here. I shared my story about always being overweight through my childhood and high school. How mortified I was to be directed, at age four, to a bigger girls' department because I needed different, as in chubby sized clothes made for bigger girls."

"Were you really heavy as a girl?" Shannon was the largest girl in the room. No one snickered or reacted to her question in a derisive way. Good for them.

"I sure wouldn't lie about something that made me feel so bad then, but also helped make me who I am today."

Aleah raised her hand. "Could you tell us more about it, please?"

"Have you ever wondered if a chair would hold you?" Talia waved an arm at their folding chairs. "None of these chairs have arms. I'd often enter a room, glance at the seating, and a minor panic attack struck if the chairs were narrow or had arms. I gauged the dimensions and wondered if I'd even fit in the available seat."

"What made you want to change by losing the weight?"

"Good question, Sasha. A few things got my attention and pointed out the time for change was right. My freshman year of college I heard skinny girls harping about gaining the notorious freshman fifteen. I didn't like my life the way it was, how could I possibly gain more weight?"

Lydia piped up. "Were you happy?"

"Absolutely not. I was tired of telling myself lies, especially at my reflection in the mirror. I now call it a God-thing that I was determined to change my world."

"How did you start?"

Talia smiled at Shannon and kept wearing the smile as she faced each girl. "I prayed first. Got on my knees, poured out my heart through a crying jag. I'd had enough and recognized that I had to cling to the Lord. Embrace God's love for me no matter how I put myself in the way. I decided to change, and then learned to accept my new self. It took well over a year. I can't tell you how wonderful it felt to embrace femininity. I felt close to being reborn as a real girl."

"I'll bet you had guys going after you." It was the first Lydia had spoken that night.

"I wasn't searching for a guy to date in college, I was looking for a good education. My motto was just lose the pounds and enjoy whatever the Lord put in front of me. No matter if it was eating right, studying as hard as I could, or my nightly runs. I just got it done."

"God's been good to you," Shannon offered.

"God is good to all of us. Every breath is a gift of grace.

The inner workings of organs, muscles, bones, and molecules make up who we are. Each and every one of us is a creation of God. Why would we be unthankful and displeased with this body that our Abba Daddy made to house us in? It's almost game time, but I want us to read Psalm chapter 139, and then I'll pray."

A cloud hovered over their game that night. They played candy match, where the kids divided a mound of colored candy into individual cups by color, two girls against two boys. Though the girls often won, maybe due to more advanced hand/eye coordination at their age, a pall of underlying tension hovered that even eating the candy didn't lift.

Had Talia messed up by talking about herself again? She'd hoped one of the girls, especially after what Sasha had said, would have spilled her feelings. Maybe they talked among themselves about what had happened with Janiyah. How could she pray for them individually if they didn't share? *And please, Lord, don't let my emotions get out of control so I turn to food again.*

Food. Her fearful, tempting drug of choice.

Chapter 7

QUIET BUT RAPID, THE PAST week had been filled with youth pastor duties. Outside the church building the following Wednesday, Cooper's heart still raced. He'd joined in with the kids on a fast-paced chance for a seat when they played a modified game of musical chairs that involved a beach ball. He'd lost his grip on the ball. Then jumped over the back of a chair almost knocking Talia to the floor. He'd blown being "it" big-time, laughed at the memory, and scratched his head.

Talia bumped his shoulder and pulled him from his zone-out. "What's so funny?"

Cooper rolled his shoulders, slanted a one-sided grin. "That idiot game."

"Hey, that's not a good adjective."

"You're right." He stopped walking and tilted his head to view her directly. "You just leave me speechless sometimes with your beauty, and make me feel like a geeky, stuttering kid. I still find it hard to believe you're not used to guys hitting on you all the time."

"Thanks." She shuffled her feet, rolled her teeth over her bottom lip. "One of the girls asked me the same thing last week. We didn't even talk about Janiyah."

"That surprises me. The guys really got into the whole theme of harming one's self due to Dustin's reference that he didn't have a parent who cared. And then there's Sasha's admission."

"We didn't talk about that at all. They wanted to know if I'd honestly been heavy. As though I'd make up such a thing. That brought on the remark about dudes hitting on me. It's always nice to receive compliments. Since I reduced in pounds, I've been suspicious of men's attention. No, guys didn't fall all over me after I dropped sizes. I just wasn't interested and brushed them off. One thought has never changed, before and after my diminished body size, because it's hard for me not to wonder about motives. In high school both girls and guys wanted me to help with homework, so I'd ask myself 'What does he want? What does she see?'"

"But it's clear to me that you've learned to accept your new physical self. You're such an attractive woman, you come off as being comfortable in your skin."

"I do embrace femininity. I like to look good. I love to move well because I exercise and eat right."

I need Your help here, Lord. Could You soften her heart toward what I'm about to say? "So you haven't spent time on building positive, healthy relationships?"

She pulled back her head like a turtle drawing into its shell. "Where did that come from?"

"I think about you way too much. I'd like to find out if whatever's between the two of us can develop into something long-lasting."

Talia's chin went forward, followed by her upper body, as though she hadn't heard right. "Wow. Are you sure? I still have body image issues." She huffed, wiggled her pretty pink-painted fingernails. "I'm tempted to abuse myself if I gain three pounds, which can happen over a single weekend. Binging and starving do not represent taking proper care of a body that's the temple of God."

"You're so right. According to First Corinthians six, our bodies house the Holy Spirit. It never abandons us. It works by God's design. He has set you apart as a masterpiece because God made the body you live in. As much as I'm sometimes dumbstruck over your amazing outer appearance, I approve of who you are inside. I think if we'd met before the weight came off, I'd still want to know you better."

"Are you sure about that?" She must need reassurance if she asked twice. "Then you'd be scoffed at for spending time with an obese woman. You'd have to put up with my mother's and sister's opinions of me. I find myself noticing other people's appearance out in public. So much of our population is overweight. Yet, I wonder about my own judgment and why society thinks it so wrong to be heavy?"

"Hear you. I take in the newscasters and can't help but think how the majority seem anorexic. Some of those women's arms look like chicken wings."

"All right, already. I need to check in early at work in the morning. Let's agree the next time we're together we don't talk about body size?" Talia swung her arm with keys extended and her Jeep door clicked.

"Remember Saturday. We have a date for the Huskers." Cooper jiggled his eyebrows.

"Oh, joy." Her laugh tinkled over him like a sweet song. "We'll join the largest Nebraska city on stadium seats. Go Big Red."

"Weather's supposed to cooperate. See you then." He needed every ounce of resistance he possessed not to jump or fist bump the air. He actually had a date with the dazzling Talia Ashby. He willed the next two days to skip by.

✞✞✞

The rambunctious college football game on Saturday turned out exactly as Talia imagined. The noisy crowd exhausted her. In contrast, the time with Cooper left her exhilarated. She hadn't gone to many games as a student because of being squished into a narrow seat, but there'd been no problem fitting in one that afternoon. She'd knocked her selfish pride to the curb, and rooted for Big Red, who had won by ten points. Drowning in Cooper's attention fed her enough that she wasn't hungry for an evening meal.

She'd actually relaxed and had fun in his company. "Thank You, Jesus. You have Your hand on all the lives of Your children. I am fine with You putting Cooper and me together according to Your will. I fully accept Your plan for our lives. Wherever Janiyah is tonight, and the rest of the kids from Southside, be with them. Draw them to Yourself and protect them. Amen."

Cookie pawed Talia's leg.

"All right." She scratched behind the golden's ears and patted her head. "I know a treat is overdue. Sorry we only got in one walk today. But you already ran around when I came home." Talia foraged treats from two separate bags in the pantry. She also fought the urge to raid the shelves for herself. She'd eaten cheesy nachos at the game, a definite no-no food item, so she'd already indulged in what she shouldn't. "God in me is more important than overeating once a week."

She sat at the table in front of the sliding doors and stared out, wishing it was warm enough to sit on the patio. Journal time.

Cookie padded over and laid her head across Talia's

thigh. "Hi there, sweet Coop—oh no, did I really start to say his name instead of yours?" She laughed and groaned at the same time. "Don't give me those sad, begging eyes."

The dog raised one eyebrow, then the other.

Talia laughed again. "Come on now, give me a break. I'm working on this week's lesson. Refocus. Rethink."

She jotted in a journal much like the ones she'd given the girls. *What's the purpose of your body? Is it all about what shows on the outside? What about how it works for you? Your brain doesn't engage your conscience as it tells your muscles when to move. Your heart beats without you thinking about it. Your eyes see. Your ears listen. Your lungs breathe. Your intestines digest food without you telling them to work. You are wonderfully and fearfully made.*

Once those words had been her mantra. Fearfully and wonderfully made. "Thank You, Abba Father for creating me."

Should she share with the girls any label size worn on the inside of clothing didn't matter? Her body, and theirs, worked as they were designed to work. According to their Maker.

Talia bowed her head. "Dear God, You created a miracle when You formed me and planned my life before my parents met. You knew me way before time began. Please show me how I can relay that mind-boggling truth to the young girls at Southside so it becomes ingrained and they don't have to suffer with outward looks the way I've struggled. Thank You, my Jesus. Amen."

The phone rang. Perfect timing. She smiled at sight of Cooper's name. How would he react over her almost calling her dog by his name? She'd better forget. "Hi, Cooper. Long time, no see."

"Funny. Hi, radiant beauty. I forgot to mention the game I've planned for Wednesday. I don't want to overspend the budget. Think the two of us could splurge on boxes of tissues?"

Radiant beauty and a box of tissues in the same breath? "You mean the blowing your nose kind?"

"Right. We need tissues for a nutty game."

"Aren't all your games nutty?" She couldn't help but tease. "You make them all kinds of silly. A bit dangerous as well."

She pictured him slapping his hand against his chest and rearing back. "Slam. Thanks for your kind assessment."

They enjoyed a laugh. They'd shared countless moments like that during the other games while the youth competed. Well, the times they could hear each other. She always knew where he was. Caught his sideways glances at her in turn.

"We can go to the dollar joint. Anyway, the kids stand around a long table and each student gets a box of tissues. When I tell 'em to 'Go!' they empty the boxes as fast as they can to see who is first and who is last. That last person gets a dumb prize, or we make him pick them all up instead. I haven't decided yet."

"I can just picture that giant pile of tissues."

They agreed on the number of boxes each would purchase and went on to talk about everything under the sun except teen issues. He caught her up on where each of his brothers lived, all married, and the ages and names of their children. She told him about an easier phone conversation with her sister Ebonee.

All of a sudden Cooper yelped.

"What?"

"Do you know what time it is?"

She checked. "Gracious. We've talked for two hours?"

"Yes, we have. Church tomorrow. Do you think the whole place would hum if we sat together?"

"Would you mind if a few tongues waggled?"

"I'd be pleased to sit with the most beautiful woman in the congregation."

"Hey, I'm not embarrassed to sit with the handsome youth pastor who makes me feel feminine. With my fat history such a thing will be a new experience." She found it hard to define how those feelings of inadequacy still raised their heads, but Cooper's presence replaced them and made her all giggly inside. Also nervous, excited, and thrilled. "I don't know what else to say, Cooper."

He waited so long to speak she wondered if one of their phones had gone dead.

Then his low, breathy voice raised shivers all over her body. "See you in the morning then, dazzling Talia."

✞✞✞

Monday and Tuesday the lyrics of Sunday's solo played through Talia's thoughts. The praise team's rendition of "Reckless Love" had been directed to the Lord. As thankful as she was for God's mercy toward her, and the fact that He gave her breath and form, she couldn't picture herself dancing with wild abandon over how God's reckless love for her had lifted her into another realm of existence.

Had God sung over her before He breathed life into her? Were the young teens, and even older congregants soaking up the lyrics? As beautiful as the words and presentation were, she'd sat stiffly in her seat. Should she question her staid behavior? Maybe she was uptight as Ebonee had often accused.

Now it was Wednesday night already, and Talia found it hard to concentrate during youth group. The kids scurried out, but Janiyah offered to help Talia clean up the room. "I don't have a ride home tonight, Miss Talia. Do you think you could take me?"

"Of course. Do you need to let your grandma know you'll get home safe?"

"She's in a meeting. Some kind of counseling before I see a head shrink for the stunt I pulled. I asked her to find out if I could just talk to you and Pastor Coop instead."

He came up from behind, placed a hand on Janiyah's shoulder, and nodded at Talia. "If that'll work with those in the know, it's fine with me. Go ahead, you two. I can finish up here."

She read encouragement in Cooper's glance. "All right then, let's head out."

Janiyah was quiet on the walk to the Jeep, maybe still embarrassed over her actions. For all Talia knew, it was a common thing for teens to snoop and be tempted by their elders' pills.

Just as she opened her mouth, a rickety loud pickup towing another truck that was in worse shape interrupted the quiet. The trucks entered the church parking lot and rolled to a stop, the log chain in between dangling loose and dragging.

The driver jumped out of the gray-blue truck in front, and yelled. "I think your clutch is burning up."

"Oh, man. I can't afford this." A tall, thin man climbed down from the passenger side of the red pickup being pulled, hopped on the bumper, and propped open the hood with its stick. Then of all things, he sat there under the hood holding a large wrench while the first driver tugged the second pickup back onto the road.

"Wow, I guess I'm not the only one with problems." Janiyah choked out a laugh.

"It's called life, girl. No one ever said it would be easy." Talia unlocked the Jeep doors. "Buckle up and we'll be on our way."

A block from the church lot they saw the pickups on a side street. The skinny guy was shouting foul language.

"That man needs Jesus. I have something to tell you, Miss Talia. First, thanks again for coming to see me in the hospital."

"You're welcome. Seeing you there gave us quite the scare. And remember, you can come to me any time."

Janiyah nodded.

"How's your grandmother's health?"

"She's better. Upset with herself for leaving her prescription bottles in plain sight, and feeling bad over what I did."

"That's understandable. She probably feels guilty because she had stuff in the medicine cabinet. Ready to tell me how you're doing?"

"To be truthful, I've had some rough days. I was just so tired of hearing the other kids in school whispering and calling me names. I hate that N word. I can't help it my skin is so dark. I was fed up. Thought I couldn't take it anymore."

"I honestly do understand." Talia nodded. "And I appreciate you being up front with me. Thanks for not saying TBH. I remember the eye rolls and whatevers if I responded to taunts when I was a girl. Hurtful words are hard to ignore."

"Kid's still say whatever, and they aren't the only ones who say to be honest, TBH. G-Ma hates it. Everyone knew about me and the pills the next day when I went back to school. The jabs came at me from all sides. They make fun of me because I'm so tall. My skin is so black. Why is my hair so short? I was sick of it all. Even after all you and Pastor Coop tell us, what I've read in the Bible, the things you've said about being opposite of me. So heavy." Janiyah heaved a sigh that spoke volumes. "Well, I wanted to end it all. I wanted to do it better the next time. Finish the job. I even researched how to commit suicide."

Talia didn't gasp aloud only through sheer force of will. Janiyah probably wouldn't care, but Talia gritted her teeth to keep silent and let the girl talk. To keep from commenting, she gripped the steering wheel with all her might.

"I clicked on the suicide link and before I saw the site, a dialog box popped up. A man with long hair and beard who looked like a street person, pointed and said what rolled across the screen in caps. JESUS LOVES YOU. At that same instant a voice in my head repeated, '*I love you. You are my precious child.*'" Tears clogged Janiyah's voice. "I almost dropped my phone."

Talia ignored the wetness on her cheeks and kept blinking to keep her gaze on the street. "His love is undeniable. He never gives up on His chosen children."

"This is my corner." Janiyah pointed. "Right away, I said out loud, 'Jesus, I know You love me. Thank You, and I'm so sorry for not believing. Forgive me.'"

"Oh, girl. Angels were singing in heaven." Talia slowed and turned the steering wheel.

"I don't think I can say how different I am inside. It's

like I've been washed clean or something. I want to smile all the time. I honestly do believe that I have a Father who cares for me. I want to let everyone know, but who can I tell that would even listen? People think I'm just a skinny black girl they can make fun of. It doesn't hurt near as much as it used to."

Talia read the house number and pulled up at the curb. She released her seat belt and turned. "May I hug you?"

Janiyah followed suit and raised her arms. Talia squeezed and Janiyah clung.

"Thank you, dear Abba Daddy, for welcoming Janiyah into Your family. Thank You that I now have a new sister in Christ. I wish a blessing on this child of Yours and ask that You show her the way she is meant to share her new life in Christ. I praise, honor, and glorify You, dear Lord. Amen."

"I'm so excited that my face might split with all this smiling." Janiyah squeezed Talia again. "My hopeless world turned full of hope. For sure, life will be hard. I know the other kids will keep saying ugly things. But I hope they see me hold up my head and that I can show them something in me they want for themselves. I want to tell them God's love makes all the difference."

"You're right. God's love makes all the difference in the world. I remember well that wonderful sensation of being washed clean from the inside out. It's a shame more of us don't keep that euphoria for times after we turn ourselves over to Jesus." Talia gave another squeeze and relaxed her arms. "I'll pray for your witness to others, Janiyah, and that you gain new friends. Take one day at a time. Read as much of the Bible as you can. Write in your journal. Talk to me, or someone, if you're feeling low."

"I'd better get inside." Janiyah opened the door, hopped out, and hesitated. "You can tell Pastor Coop if you want."

"That will be my pleasure. But first. Be assured you're not the only one who has troubles."

"Like those guys in the trucks. It's good you can understand, Miss Talia. It's good to know someone cares."

"I do care. Most importantly, God cares. Good night, Janiyah."

"See ya."

Talia grabbed her phone and texted Cooper. *Are you still at the church?*

No immediate answer, so he must be driving home.

She started up and headed to her place. An old sing-song rhyme came out of nowhere. *I don't want her. You can have her. She's too fat for me.*

"Get behind me, Satan." Though her hands shook and her stomach curled, she sang the favored hymn, "Jesus loves me."

She prayed and sang all the way home. She could hardly stand waiting to call Cooper as soon as she got inside. The new and neat, cookie-cutter patio houses on her street were all the same except for the siding color. Would she ever have a personalized home, maybe one with a porch? And what was wrong with imagining a white picket fence? Not the lifestyle of millennials, for sure.

She'd much rather dream than revisit ugly words that surfaced from the past. Or dwell on her reluctance to saddle Cooper with another woman who had issues when it came to food.

Chapter 8

"DREAM BIG AND LIVE WITH purpose for God's glory." Talia laughed out loud. "God, I love Your surprises."

She slowed for her driveway. Her chest bounced with joy at sight of Cooper's yellow ride sitting outside her place. That's why he hadn't answered her call. He waited for her in person.

He waved, drew himself up and out of the sports car, and patted the back fender as the garage door whirred up. "Hey, dazzling beauty."

Her thanks came out on a giggle. "It's been so long since I saw you. And it's a good thing I know you."

"Sure. A stalker would never park a yellow rig next to your curb."

"Rig, ha. That pint-sized speedster?" She swung out and addressed Cookie through the closed door. "Yes, I'm home. Hang on. We've got company."

"I saw her playing with the curtain at the front window. I didn't hear her bark."

"She doesn't bark much."

"What do you do for a guard dog then?"

His obvious concern hit her soul-deep. "I take precautions. Besides, Cookie's good company and I love her."

"Okay, but Lincoln's grown so much we can't be too careful in any part of town." He smiled that familiar grin from years before and didn't follow her onto the wide stoop. "It's such a nice night. You go let her do her business or whatever, and I'll wait for you out here."

Talia took care of Cookie and within five minutes, joined him at the tiny iron patio table outside her front door.

Cookie leaped up and licked his chin.

"Down, girl. Sit."

The dog obeyed him.

Talia hooked the leash around an iron chair leg. "Okay."

Cookie swirled in a flurry of curls and laid her chin on Talia's leg. The pup raised her eyes so far into her scraggly hair it looked like she had no eyelids.

Cooper laughed. "I get why you love her."

Talia hoped the golden glow from the outside light didn't reveal her blush. "She is so energetic, and way too friendly. I have yet to get her not to jump on other people."

"Maybe I should visit more often and you can use me to train her."

"I think I'd like that." Nothing to think about, if he meant what she thought he did. As in the dating kind of visits.

"So would I, if it's all right with you. The propriety thing, though. Me a single pastor and you living alone. I won't go past your living room, just to avoid any nosy window peepers."

Oh my. The onslaught of such respect drained the starch right out of her, and she sagged in her seat like a rag doll. As a girl, she'd strenuously longed to be treated in such a way. Her world would have been different.

"Are you that worn out from running Janiyah home?"

She sat tall, waved a hand in the air is if to clear it. "Not at all. Your kindness took out my stuffing. Are you saying what I think you are about visiting us often?"

He skimmed her fingertips with his. The rougher texture of his fingers grazed between hers, over the knuckles, and then rasped the skin above her wrist bone. He turned her hand over and placed two light-as-a breath kisses on the underside.

She forgot her name.

"You are the epitome of femininity."

His touch on her hand muddled her thoughts. "I'm positive you're repeating yourself."

"I'd think feeling feminine is a world above the sense of being a blob, which is all in your past. I don't care for hearing you put yourself down."

The gravity of his gaze grilled the edges of her heart.

"I want to get to know the woman you are now. I've always caught your humor, always known you're smarter than me. Now I'd like to catch you before some other guy finds you as attractive as I do."

"Catch me like a fish?"

"I'm not joking at all, Talia." His voice broke. He kissed her wrist again.

What if he found her lacking, the way she'd not been acknowledged all her life? *I'm not worthy of Cooper's attention.* Would he hurt her the way everyone else had? Should she let him in?

"Why do you smell so good? I'd say it's intoxicating, but I've never been drunk. Getting close to you tempts me, and I love fragrances." He inhaled, pulled her hair to the front, and gathered it between his fingers. "Do you use lemon shampoo? You're so hard to resist on Wednesdays. After you take off with the girls, I can still smell you in the room at church."

Talk about intoxicating. "Uh. Grapefruit. Grapefruit on my hair. I also wear patchouli. I hope it isn't too strong because it can be. I have it in my closet and mix it in my unscented body lotion." She knocked herself in the forehead with her fingertips. "Way too much information. Sorry. You could talk a sled dog into eating snow."

"Never. Thanks for trusting me enough to spill." He drew back slowly. "I'd love to kiss you right now. It takes superhuman strength to resist you."

"This is all new to me, Cooper. So many changes. Attending Southside, working with the girls, being around you again. I'm having a hard time facing old ghosts, as in insecurities. I—"

He closed her mouth with a finger. "Shh. As much as I'm dazzled by your physical appearance, and the way you give of yourself to the girls, I want you to know how I feel. I'm pretty sure I'm falling in love with you."

She fisted the bottom of her shirt to keep herself from jumping into his arms. Not one person had ever said those words to her. Crazy, the way she longed for love, and someone to cherish her. What would it be like if she let him care for her as long as she'd let him? What if he knew she'd never been kissed? Was she even worth kissing, especially with the chance she'd get bigger some day?

She'd never seen him sit so still, his gaze riveted on her eyes, waiting.

And she had no clue what to say.

✝✝✝

In his garage workshop, Cooper replayed the conversation with Talia. He should have waited. Should have prayed before he declared his feelings. Given her more time. Did she really deal with lifelong issues relevant to body size? As much as he didn't want to admit it, he doubted he would have fallen for her had she still been overweight. That didn't say a whole lot for his character. Then again, he'd always loved his mother no matter if she was large or her present smaller self.

Smaller self. Immediately he pictured Analise and hit his finger with the hammer. He may be building something as small as a birdhouse, but he needed to pay attention in the presence of his tools rather than get lost in his head. He pounded in the nail with one zap and set aside the hammer.

Absently, he ran a finger over the scar on his forearm caused when a hacksaw blade snapped. If he could so easily graze the emotional scars due to the loss of his only sister. So smart. So talented. Why had she abused her body in such a way? He'd never understood. She sang like a lark but gave up singing in church. She was almost as lovely as Talia, only not in an exotic way.

He strode at a fast clip back and forth in front of the workbench. Was he turning over-protective concerning Talia due to guilt over losing his sister? Had he let down Talia and Janiyah over her suicide attempt? How he'd treated Analise had come crashing into him at the hospital at the door of Talia's room. He'd been in a similar room years earlier where he was slammed with the feeling his parents had loved him and his brothers second-best, after Analise. The irony was she hadn't died due to an eating disorder.

Cooper ceased his long strides and dug his fingers into his temples at the resurrected scene from the past, accentuating his guilt.

He'd been so ashamed of his sister's emaciation that he

avoided her at a shopping mall. Later, he'd ignored her when she waved from a carousel. He was as guilty as kids who openly mocked others due to their physical appearance. Her sickly appearance embarrassed him in front of his friends, so he'd pretended he didn't know her in public.

"Lord, forgive me. Help me make it up to the memory of Analise by doing something for another person to lift them up." How could he ever admit such a thing to Talia? That kind of confession could make her relive the angst she'd suffered due to her younger days of being scorned due to her weight.

His phone rang and pulled him from his ugly thoughts.

Burke, one of the youth group boys. He'd vowed to himself when he took the position as youth pastor that he'd be available to the kids or their family members at any time, even 10:45 PM. "Hey, Burke, what's up?"

"I, I need to talk to someone, Pastor Coop."

"I'm here." He opened the inside garage door and shut out the light. "Can we do it over the phone or do you need to see me?"

"Uh, the phone is good." Burke's voice shook and squeaked from low to high. "I've seen something I shouldn't have."

Oh, boy. That could be anything. Cooper popped a cup of coffee he hadn't tossed that morning into the microwave. "Go on. Take your time."

"I was at my friend's house. Walked by his mom's room. She was undressing." Cooper heard the anguish in the boy's voice. "She smiled at me and stripped right out of her clothes. I was like frozen in place."

"I'm sure that was awkward."

"She didn't even close the door. And I couldn't move. Like, I was a statue. Then she motioned for me to enter." He choked. "I, I couldn't. I ran back to my friend's room."

Cooper grabbed his coffee. He hated the painful tears in the boy's voice. "Did you tell him what happened?"

"How could I? And how can I ever run into his mom again without seeing her naked in my mind?"

"I can tell how upset you are, Burke. Why don't you close your eyes and take some deep breaths while I pray?" Cooper followed his own suggestion and paced in front of the breakfast bar. "Lord Jesus, we come before You now with a heartfelt plea. Burke is hurting. He doesn't understand what just happened, and I'm really sorrowful that he had this experience. Please impress upon him that he's not at fault. He was taken advantage of by someone who should know better. We're human. We all fall short, dear heavenly Father, we all sin. I pray that You comfort Burke now, be with him, draw him closer to You, and help him have a good night's sleep. In Your precious name, we pray, amen."

"Thanks." Burke's voice was barely audible through his tears.

With a heavy heart, Cooper sipped his now tepid coffee. The only light came from digital readings and filtered through the window from the street, outlining the furnishings. The dim shadows accented the depth of his care for these kids who lived in a dark world.

✞✞✞

Thursday evening the garage door rolled down behind her as Talia exited her Jeep. She smiled at the familiar thump of Cookie's paws on the utility room door. The pup staved off loneliness.

Her phone rang just as she reached for her boisterous pup. "Hello?"

"Hi, Miss Talia. This is Shannon. Uh. From youth group?"

"Sure, Shannon. What can I do for you?"

"Well, I've been thinking about some of the stuff you've been telling us and, um…you can see I'm not skinny so I was wondering if you could maybe help me eat better?"

"Shannon, I'm honored that you're trusting me with your request. I only now walked in from work. If you don't mind a few distracting noises, I need to let out my dog and unload a few things, then I'll be happy to listen to anything that's on your mind."

"Go ahead. You've told us, and I know there's a Bible verse that says God sees into the heart. But I'm so much bigger than the other girls my age, I feel huge and out of place most of the time."

Talia pictured Shannon. She was broad shouldered and wide-hipped, but she had a trim waist and long legs. "The first thing I'll say is that you probably had a growth spurt or two, and the other girls haven't had theirs yet. It's the same as our walk with God, our spiritual walk. That is, we all grow at a different pace. And for the record, you have a body proportion that in a couple years the other girls will be envious of. I've always wished I was taller, I had to work to get the waist and legs I have now."

"Exercise makes sense, but it's hard to believe you worked that hard. I feel so clumsy and huge. Kids stare at me." Her voice hiccupped. "I've been called elephant and moose and hippo."

"I hear you. I've been there. I understand about being

called names and hearing nonstop fat jokes. But earlier than that, in elementary school, I was called things like Ashy Tail, Tall Ashes that turned into a pile of ashes. If I tried to say anything back, the taunting worsened." She opened the door and Cookie leaped onto the patio.

"I can text you a few websites that point to healthy food choices. I'll also help you learn to identify emotional triggers for overeating, which destroy creative, intuitive healthy living."

"I'd like that." Shannon's voice sounded brighter.

"Don't embrace who you think you are or aren't based on the opinions of other kids. Rather, consider who you are in Christ. Write those affirmations in your journal. Celebrate life, embrace being a girl, take advantage of your uniqueness, your gifts and talents. You have leadership qualities that I'm guessing God will use to help others as you go forward."

"You really think so, Miss Talia?"

"I know so. God always knew His plan for me and the journey I've been on. He has a plan for you also, and everyone you know. Remember that you're never alone."

"Man, being a girl is hard."

Talia couldn't help but smile. "God never promised life would be easy for boys or girls. Embrace the obstacles. Don't look at situations as problems, but opportunities to learn and grow."

"You're so smart. Thank you for listening and making me feel better."

"God's power makes the weak strong." She let in the pup, which ran crazily around the room sliding on the slick wood floor. "Call on His power to make you strong." Talia needed to follow her own advice, dig into her journals for areas of life the Lord had already brought her through. "Life is not fair. Life is not perfect. People aren't perfect. God gives you the ability to power through. He'll make you strong."

Shannon yawned.

"You know, there's a walk coming up that focuses on eating disorders. I'm not saying you have one. I'm taking longer walks to prepare for that event. Do you think the other girls in youth group would like to learn about healthy food preparation? I could reserve the church kitchen." She stopped. "Just listen to me carry on."

"I think you're an angel, Miss Talia. Yes, I want to learn good food choices from you."

She'd do almost anything to ease the pain of life for these girls. She was a prime example of falling short, according to her mother and sister, who'd both influenced Talia in negative ways that still weighed on her.

Chapter 9

COOPER CLAPPED HIS HANDS AND and shut the classroom door. His head count assured him the youth were all present. "Hey, everyone. Happy Wednesday night. We're changing things up by starting on a light note, as in playing a game first. Remember all those tissues we pulled out of boxes? Well, we kept those boxes and will tie them around our waists. Miss Talia and I will join you."

She turned to Shannon. "Please help me pass a box to everyone."

The girl eagerly jumped up.

"Girls, pair off and let's tie the boxes around each other's waist. Try not to spill the balls that are inside." Cooper swept his arm in an arc. "Guys, help each other and be kind about it."

He held onto the ends of the cord strung through a box and placed it around Talia. The grapefruit scent of her hair tempted him to move it aside and kiss her ear. Instead, he whispered, "I'll bet I've got more junk in my past to shake off than you do."

She shoved away his hands without making eye contact and tied on his box.

He wished he could keep touching her. "All right, attention, please. When I say go, line up in two rows. Any order. The object is to shake the bouncy balls out of the tissue boxes. We all drag around baggage behind us. That means unresolved hurts and guilt. So let's shake it off."

Cooper counted off on his fingers. "One, two, three. Go!"

Amidst wild laughter and crazy hip movements, everyone twisted and jived until the boxes were empty. Talia won. Sasha was second, and Ransom third.

"We'll pick up the balls in a bit. Leave them on the floor for now and try not to step on them. Everyone find a seat. Keep your empty boxes tied around your waists."

Talia gave him a quizzical look along with the students, and then perched on the end of a chair.

"I'm reminding you of a Bible story from the Old Testament. Who knows the story of Joseph?"

Most of the hands raised or popped up and then down.

"Joseph had quite a life. His brothers were jealous because he was favored by their father. So they sold him. Because of the talents and intelligence God gave him, even as a slave, Joseph earned the highest position in Egypt besides that of pharaoh. I want to talk about how he was tempted by Potiphar's wife in Genesis chapter thirty-nine." Cooper glanced at Talia. No way would he make eye contact with Burke.

"Now, I'm guessing most of you have been exposed to sights on social media that would have made my mother blush and my father's mouth drop open."

A couple of the boys fidgeted. Two raised their heads as if a puppeteer had jerked them upward and kept their focus on the opposite wall.

"I know girls are dared, even bullied into flashing." He gave them a moment to get out of their thoughts and pay attention, glancing at individuals from time to time. "At one point, Joseph went to wealthy Potiphar's house to do business and found no man there. But the wife was home. She wanted to get Joseph in her bed and grabbed his clothing. Joseph did the manly, and godly thing. He ran. He let her pull off his garment and he raced from the home. No way would he allow himself to be pulled into sin. Does anyone remember what happened?"

Lydia raised her hand. "Potiphar's wife accused Joseph of assaulting her, and he was put in prison."

"That's correct. He was falsely accused, but his heart was free from guilt because he hadn't fallen into sin." Cooper bent and picked up a red bouncy ball, tossed if from hand to hand. "You might wonder what this story has to do with us today. Well, it proves that integrity is rewarded. By doing the right thing, by running from temptation without a second thought, God honors our decisions. It's okay to say no. It doesn't matter if friends make fun of us for not hooting over dirty pictures or reading stories that don't honor doing the right thing. If any girl is asked to show herself, she needs to immediately ignore the request and seek help from an adult. Miss Talia, do you have anything to add?"

Her shoulder jerked, but she recovered in a flash. "We're all tempted. I'm not that much older than you, but I know you've seen things I probably have never looked at, just because social media has made such things available. If you're tempted, thinking only a couple people are involved, you'd be wrong. Turn and just run the way Joseph did. Later, block that contact. God will honor your choice. And if you do take a peek, go right to the Lord. Ask forgiveness right away. Don't let repeated thoughts or dirty images fester like rotten food wrappers or garbage chasing around in your head."

"Or boxes on your butts." Leave it to Ransom for comic relief.

✝✝✝

"I'm not going to elaborate on what Pastor Cooper brought up with you all." Talia faced the circle of girls. "But, please, if you're ever asked to show body parts on social media or anything else that makes you feel violated, ask someone for help. Especially if it's an adult making the request. You are never at fault."

She waited for the nervous body movements to still. "I began my journal entry today with a Bible verse. In Philippians 1:6, Paul says, 'He,' meaning God, 'began a good work in me.' Also in each of you. He will complete it. He made each and every one of us. If God made us, we are worthy in His eyes. He loves us. He'll never give up on you or me. I know I fail Him every single day. We all do because we were born sinners. But He'll work in our hearts and lives until our dying day. Only then, when we see Jesus face to face, will we be perfect."

"Don't we have to invite Jesus in to do that work, once what we read in the Bible is clear to us?"

"Yes, Lydia. That's exactly right. As soon as the Holy Spirit grants us understanding, it's up to us to receive God's love. God is gracious and offers us that choice."

"Is it a sin if we don't?" Aleah played with her ponytail.

"That's where second chances come in. God gives us second chances over and over. But there also comes a point where God can turn His back if we've had umpteen opportunities and continually turn to darkness. He'll give us up to Satan." *Help me out here, Lord. I don't think I should have said that.* Talia cleared her voice and smiled. "I believe that happens later in life. For now, girls, you're all young and God's got you covered."

"Thanks, Miss Talia." Janiyah wiped the corner of her eye. "You had me scared there for a sec."

"I apologize for that. Do any of you have questions? I just thought we'd chat tonight. If you have biblical questions, Pastor Cooper is the one to go to, but I'll always try."

The girls squiggled in their chairs, made faces, two scribbled.

Sasha raised her hand. "My grandmother says that the eyes are the windows of the soul. I'm not sure I understand what that means."

"Ah. That quote comes from William Shakespeare."

"Romeo and Juliette and all those plays older kids complain they have to study." Shannon made a goofy face that drew titters.

"Right. This might be something to jot down in your journals. I'm not sure our soul is revealed in our eyes, but maybe our thoughts and emotions. Mood or health, is for sure. I believe Matthew wrote about it. If you have an index or concordance, turn to the backs of your Bibles."

"I've got it." Lydia held up a hand and read from her Bible. "Matthew 6:22-23. 'The eye is the lamp of the body. If your eyes are healthy, your whole body will be full of light. But if your eyes are unhealthy, your whole body will be full of darkness. If then the light within you is darkness, how great is that darkness!' Wow. Does that mean if we're bad it shows in our eyes?"

"Good job. I'm sure it can sometimes, but what you think shows might be your own guilt. The same as happiness not only shows in a smile, but when we're joyful it spreads to reflect in our eyes. You can light up the world around you." She laughed and raised her eyes to the ceiling.

"My grandmother told me about a popular song in her time that was called *You Light Up My Life*. That person who comes to mind can be a mother, a friend, or Jesus. No matter who you consider the light in your life, it will show in your eyes and through your smile. And when you connect with others, look into their eyes and see the beauty of their souls."

"How can that light be seen, Miss Talia?" Janiyah sat straighter.

"Yeah." Aleah nodded. "Troubles can suck all the good out of a day. How do we change what we focus on?"

"I have to pray about that. Just for fun, notice your friends this coming week. Search their eyes. Try to figure out if their hearts are filled with radiance, illness, or sadness. You can smile and be that light of Jesus to someone who is having a hard day. A true smile is revealed in our eyes."

Lydia giggled. "Is that why Pastor Coop has so many lines by his eyes? Cause he smiles so much?"

"Could be." Talia returned a grin. "Let's not ask him, okay?"

A beat of silence rang loud as Janiyah's long sigh resounded in the small room. "I don't know how I can help someone else when it's hard for me not to have a dark day."

"It says a lot that you can ask, and I'm sure there are others wondering the same thing. It's not easy. I have tough days too." Talia thanked the Lord not one girl appeared bored or distracted. "The first thing that works for me is to be thankful. Just say the first thing that pops into your mind. I'm thankful I didn't have a pop quiz today. I'm thankful my jeans were clean. I'm thankful my mom is a good cook."

"Does that really work?" Shannon asked. "You make it

sound easy."

"It does work. Some days I have to work at it harder than others. Having a grateful heart becomes second nature after a while."

Aleah raised her hand. "Give us more examples."

"You can change your viewpoint by thinking of someone other than yourself. That friend whose eyes showed sadness or weren't clear. Maybe she's ill. Could be a friend complimented you on something as silly as the shade of your lipstick, remember how that made you feel. It made you happy. Smile about it. Soak it in and grin. Dance a little bit. And then, find a way to extend that kindness to someone else."

The room grew quiet.

Talia sought help from the Lord for how to proceed. "Have you ever heard of a popcorn prayer?"

The girls answered no or shook their heads.

"It's when we bow our heads, not looking up or at anyone, and just pop out with what's on our hearts. You don't have to say anything unless the Lord prompts you. If something comes to mind, pray. Do it even if your heart pounds in your ears. I'll start." She bowed her head. "Thank You, Lord, for being the best Teacher ever."

"I thank You for never giving up on me."

Talia waited through a beat of silence. "Thanks for the many promises in the Bible, such as the fact that You will never leave us nor forsake us."

"Thank you for being patient when I make dumb mistakes."

"Thanks for Miss Talia and Pastor Cooper."

"I thank you for this church."

"Thank you for friends."

"Thanks for the games with the boys, even if some of them are stupid."

A snort followed that one. Shannon must have been referring to all the crazy dances and jerky moves as they'd bounced balls out of empty tissue boxes. "There were balls all over the room, but thanks for helping us girls empty our boxes first."

Talia agreed. The room grew quiet. "Thank you for the privilege of praying to You, Lord. I thank you for each of these girls, and even the boys that are here tonight." Talia waited for the inevitable chuff of a laugh. "In Your name, Jesus. Amen."

The door opened to let them know the boys were finished.

"Oh, good." Talia agreed with Sasha's relief.

"I'm hangry." Aleah's slang gave the girls freedom to release energy. They scurried to rejoin the boys.

Cooper's silly suggestion of scooping up those bouncy balls by using cups instead of hands proved an apt release for the heavy topics of the night. Invisible waves of tension rolled off the kids.

She left the room with Cooper and they exited the building. Once outside, they shook off their tension of the previous ninety minutes by blowing heavy, tension-relieving twin exhalations.

"I sure hope we can lighten up our time together next week. We had a heavy discussion after what you introduced." She swung her shoulder into his.

"You're telling me. I don't know about girls, but stats reveal that by the time boys are twelve, they've seen on social media what God intended for married couples to regard as holy."

"I hate this sad world we live in, Cooper. In my former church a couple married guys got into pornography. One repented. The other wouldn't give it up and his addiction ended in divorce. His wife was so ashamed that she moved away."

He swung an arm around her waist and pulled her in close. Her purse bounced between them. He swept it behind them. "What's church security to think of us playing hanky-panky in the parking lot?"

"Hanky-panky is right." She swung her purse to the outside arm and adjusted the strap. Much better. She sidled closer against his side. "The girls aren't crazy about your games, but I'll hand it to you for using those tissue boxes as a valid object lesson."

"I don't know where I get ideas sometimes. As crazy as I can act, I do try to listen to the Spirit."

"You're doing fine, Cooper." At her Jeep door, she started to pull away from him. His efforts caused her to love him more. And it scared her. Was she good enough for him, suitable to share a pastor's life?

He planted both hands on her hips. "I could use a favor, if you wouldn't mind. I need to get more organized. It seems I waste a lot of time planning a game and lesson notes in readiness for Wednesdays with those kids."

"I'm the world's worst secretary."

"Oh, I don't mean that. I'm asking if you'll pray for me. This pastor stuff is hard because I'm such a kid at heart." He leaned his forehead against hers. "What if I mess up? What if one of these boys goes down the wrong track with all they're exposed to these days?"

"God will take care of us all. Of course, I already pray for you, but I'll be more specific. Your concern to be a good leader proves your sense of responsibility. I feel the same way about the girls. Kids grow up way too fast, and we have to reach them before the world turns them from the church."

"That's what I'm talking about. I wonder if I'm up to the task. No matter the age, all people need the Lord."

"We all have doubts at times, Cooper." Janiyah popped into her head. "Oh, we've been so involved with this dark stuff. I forgot to tell you about something wonderful that's happened."

He held eye contact the whole time she related how the girl came to Jesus. Rather, the way Jesus reached Janiyah.

"Praise the Lord." Cooper pulled her close and they hugged for a long time.

His need reached out to Talia on a cellular level. Was *she* up to the task the Lord put before them guiding these young people in the way they should go?

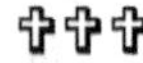

Chapter 10

TALL GLASS OF WATER IN hand, Talia wandered around her place searching for something to occupy her time. Where had the last two months gone? Since it was fall break and school was out for the week, youth group wasn't meeting. She'd already taken Cookie on a long walk. That thought made Talia laugh out loud. Leading Cookie wasn't the case at all. These days, the pup took her on a walk, more aptly, a run.

She entered the pantry and studied the food stocked on her shelves while downing the water. Within a moment, she sensed her heart rate lower as her gaze tracked healthy food choices. Shannon had expressed her wish to eat better, even learn how to prepare her own meals. Did Talia need to check with Cooper about having the girls come to her kitchen for a cooking night? Or, maybe on a Saturday? Were there rules about such a thing, as in a preference of doing meal prep in the church kitchen instead of a leader's home?

Her phone sounded from the island that divided the kitchen from the dining and living areas. She picked up on the second ringtone. "Hey, Cooper. Are you at loose ends like I am tonight?"

"You could say that." The edge to his voice sounded serious. "I'm in your driveway and we need to talk."

Talia turned on the outside light and opened her door.

Cooper pocketed his phone and reached for her upper

arm as he stepped inside.

"Can I get you anything to drink?"

Cookie raced up and leaped on Cooper. "Hi, there, sweet girl. I love you, too, but down. Sit."

The pup immediately plopped on her haunches, looked up through her long hair with pleading liquid eyes.

"I don't know how to get her to stay down when she greets people. She's just so loving." Talia locked the door, squinted her eyes, and then made a face. "Habit. Come in and have a seat."

"I'd rather stand. And thanks, but I just had my cherry PC Concoction. With caffeine." One side of his mouth lifted in a poor smile imitation. He patted Cookie. "Are all goldendoodles gray in color?"

"No. They're varied. Anywhere from an orange brown to cream or black or two or three colors combined."

Talia stepped away and slid her phone back on the mottled onyx counter. "What's wrong, Cooper? Has something happened? You're not here to talk about dogs."

He gazed at her face briefly, and then took in the open space. His attention landed back on her while he scrubbed a hand through his unruly hair. "Shannon's in the hospital."

"Where? I'll get my purse."

He stalled her with a hand on her forearm. "No."

"You're scaring me, Cooper. What happened?" She clung to his large, callused hand.

"Her mother contacted me. Shannon passed out during a long run this afternoon. A cruising police officer saw her where she'd collapsed and gave her a ride home. Then he suggested a trip to the ER. The girl has been eating little and was dehydrated so she needed fluids. They'll keep her overnight."

"Why can't I go see her?"

Cooper squeezed her hand and ran a thumb across her palm, circling back and forth. Soothing his nervousness or in an attempt to calm her?

"I'm sorry, Talia. But Shannon's mom blames you. The girl has not only starved herself, but she's worked out two hours a day. Her mother took Shannon's phone because she wanted to see you, but her mom called me instead. She asked me to tell you she doesn't appreciate your interference. She hopes it's just a phase Shannon is going through, but one that points to your influence."

"How did you and I miss this? I've paid no attention except to notice her refusal of treats on Wednesday nights."

"I've been blind as well. How was I to know Shannon was making herself ill?"

"I feel so bad, Cooper."

"I've got a hug if you think it will help."

She welcomed his arms around her and tightened her hold around his ribs. The freshness of the outdoors still clung to his hair. His strength and comfort swept over her, replaced by rising desire.

The thought popped her eyes open and ratcheted up her pulse. She wanted to kiss him. She put space between them and raised her hand to his face.

Cooper's eyes were closed as though he relished her touch. He leaned into her hand. After a beat, he moaned and reached up to remove her hand. Then he set both his hands at her waist and pushed.

"Coop?"

His piercing blue eyes drilled into her. "You tempt me, woman. That's why I never wanted to step inside your door or be alone with you in private."

She tried to smile but backed up against the wall, putting four feet between them. "I understand. What do we do about Shannon?"

"Pray, of course. I listened to her mother, but I wouldn't accept her complaint about you. I told her my sister had an eating disorder and apologized for not recognizing any clues that Shannon was in trouble. I also said that despite what you had shared about eating healthy, you couldn't be held responsible for her daughter's choices."

"Thank you for standing up for me. But I've failed somewhere along the line. I've let you down as well. And the other girls. I need to dedicate myself to all of you on a deeper level. Pray more." *And not dream about the afterward time with Cooper as well as further ahead to the extent of a future with him.*

"No way have you disappointed. You're terrific with those girls. It can't be easy. You've set aside your comfort zone to mentor them."

"But I failed Shannon, and who knows who else. My Wednesdays have turned into a teenage crush and concentration on my time with you rather than my evenings guiding the girls. I think we need to chill."

She opened the door and gave him no choice but to leave. With the door between them, she charged to the pantry. She swiped off the light switch and slammed the door, resting her head against the solidity of the smooth walnut. "Pitiful. Even after losing eighty pounds, I'm weak and angry and head right to the food."

Talia opened the refrigerator and selected a container of mixed color, bite-sized tomatoes. She filled a glass with water and ambled to the table.

Cookie bounced up and went to her side.

"Sorry, girl. I've given you a cherry tomato before and you didn't like it. Taste or texture, I don't know." She twirled a golden sphere between her fingers. "Why am I still afraid I'll lose control, gain weight, be devalued and rejected? Miss out on the relationships I have at work and church because friends would be embarrassed to hang with a fatty?"

She concentrated on chewing, relished the popping seeds, the juice, and savored the vitamin C. Once finished with her snack, she tidied up and then went to her closet to ready clothes for work the next day. Her wardrobe may be a little over the top, slim-fitting and classy, but each day she entered the hospital she determined to be as put together as possible. She loved to wear clothes that showed off her fitness and style, set off by colorful scarves or sheer kimonos, as much as she abhorred the way obesity had forced her to cover what was inside by voluminous sweaters or flowing shirts.

Perfection was impossible, be it on the inside or outside, but she relished compliments. Especially from Cooper on Sunday mornings. He'd never asked her about adding color to her black and white choices. Sure, bright colors were happy. Oh, what was she doing? Cooper had turned into more than an old crush, or her defender from way-back. By getting closer to him as they mentored youth, she'd reached beyond her comfort zone, found where the Lord could use her.

She'd always been attracted to Cooper, but his profession as a youth pastor, his gift with kids, pulled her away from those teen feelings and it was now clear. He'd made her think deeper and broader, shown how good the two were together, and she'd fallen hard. No other way to say it. Talia Ashby loved Cooper Valiant. Fine time for the realization, after she'd told Cooper they needed to spend less time alone together. It'd be next to impossible to chill the ever-rising flames of attraction.

✝✝✝

Chill. His mother had told him that his whole life. Cooper couldn't remember the last time he'd been so down. Just when he was sure God had provided the woman to stand by his side as co-minister as well as helpmeet, she put the skids on things. Maybe he was as much to blame as she was, the way his mind drifted and his heart raced so fast he could hardly wait for the meetings with Talia once the kids left the church building.

He sought the Lord's strength as he parked in a clergy slot at the hospital. Inside, Shannon's hospital room door was ajar and the light dim. An IV dripped into her arm. He entered to hear only the quiet click of some monitor. She and her mother, who was curled up in a recliner, both slept. Rather than disturb them, Cooper back-pedaled into the hallway light and scribbled a note on a youth devotional he'd grabbed from the car.

He left it on a tray in Shannon's room and prayed as he headed toward the elevator. *Sorry, Lord, if the relief I feel is wrong. I'm pretty wrecked after the emotional embrace with Talia tonight. You know what's going on in Shannon's body and mind just as you know her mother's thoughts. Please help her forgive Talia and come to different conclusions as to what's happened. We all need to forgive, Lord.*

At home he unlocked his door, sought time in the Word and prayer, unable to not contrast the exuberant greeting he'd received from Talia and her dog earlier to the stillness of his home that engulfed him now. "I won't give up! Lord, you have a purpose for bringing us back into one another's life. Show me the way. I want to be thankful in this circumstance the way James encourages in the Bible. The way Paul points out joy in Philippians. Help me."

Cooper spent thirty minutes in the Bible, and he jotted notes for his next time with the youth. Often, his thoughts ran faster than his pen. *Negative self-talk is like spam in your inbox. Irritating, worthless, nonproductive. Gaze into the mirror at your eyes, not the zit on your forehead or your nose or ears or hair that you've never liked. Talk to yourself by saying your name, remember that God knows that name and that He made you. Speak out loud whatever is bothering you, then tell yourself it doesn't change who you are. You are a being God created. He gave you breath. Thank Him for the day, for your troubles, for the strength you have now by calling upon Him.*

Everyone messed up, including himself. Sometimes being kind came easier. He needed to accept others the way he'd had no qualms about not taking Shannon's mother's complaints seriously concerning Talia. He absorbed hurt. It was harder to express kindness to himself. The way he was still bothered by his behavior, his embarrassment regarding Analise's physical appearance. He wanted to teach the youngsters that they should learn from their mistakes and be thankful for another day to find joy in living.

Your sins are as far as the east is from the west.

"What would I do without Your presence, Lord? The gift of the Holy Spirit? I can't do this leading on my own. I can't imagine a life without Talia. And now she's been hurt because she cares. A lot. The burden is heavy. I know I'm supposed to be an image bearer of Christ. Help me remember that the unchurched and everyone I meet see me as Your representative. Sometimes I might be the only avenue to what Jesus is all about that'll show up in their lives."

He'd messed up with Talia by expressing his love too early, enough that she admitted she had feelings for him. But she didn't want to pursue time with him. The weight of responsibility drove him to his knees. "Lord, I'm seeking You first, Your kingdom and Your righteousness, as stated in Matthew 6:33. I'm asking that all the heaviness on my heart will be worked out according to Your all-knowing will. One of the things on my heart is Talia. I'm becoming more and more attracted to her. That takes focus off the ministry."

Cooper wiped tears off his cheeks. "Shannon's part of that ministry. You know better than anyone what it's like for girls who aren't eating or harming themselves by overeating. Just the thought hurts me to the core because of Analise. Why can't I get over what that did to the family? Her anorexia wasn't about me. But it made me mad because Mom and Dad devoted so much time to her care. And it still tears me up the way Analise died a week after I snubbed her at the mall. Forgive me for being ashamed of her emaciated appearance."

His past actions proved that he wasn't good enough, which was obvious the way his parents expressed how they had loved Analise more than him. No wonder Talia wanted to slow things down. He wasn't worth loving.

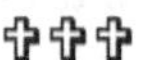

Chapter 11

CHRISTMAS DAY ALREADY. DECEMBER HAD flown by with the flurry of activities, especially at church and work get-togethers. Soft, huge snowflakes drifted across the windshield as Talia drove from the east side of Lincoln to the northwest.

She pulled into her mother's driveway, mesmerized by the shapes of the crystals now forming and sizzling on the hood. She'd been at loose ends without Cooper, the same as on Thanksgiving Eve, due to no activities at the church over the holidays. Cooper had gone to Kansas to spend Christmas with his family and warned that his brothers would keep him so busy it'd be late at night before he'd touch base with her. Despite her request to not spend time alone, they'd talked on the phone and flirted for well over an hour the night before.

Trepidation due to the usual put-downs from Mom and Ebonee built into a hard knot in Talia's stomach. They hadn't understood how or why she'd abandoned them Thanksgiving Day by volunteering in a soup kitchen. Spending the day next to Cooper as they served the homeless, though they had been far from alone, eased the bite of numerous texts and voice mails from her family that had blown up her phone.

At the swish of her sister closing the living room curtain, she knew it was time to climb out of her Jeep and carry in a broccoli-kale-Brussels sprouts salad. Warmth of the house contrasted sharply with the cold. Talia wiped her feet on the rug. Ebonee must have raced from the front window to the kitchen, where she now stood shoulder-to-shoulder, working with Mom.

"Merry Christmas to you both. I'll set my salad next to the fridge and be right back with the flavored water."

"Oh, we don't need—"

"But I made—"

She shut the door on their twin protests. No matter how hard she tried, whatever Talia did was wrong in the eyes of her mother and sister. Why was she setting herself up again for the usual scene of comparisons and put-downs?

"This must be another one of those diet foods that you'll just take home," Mom announced upon Talia's return.

Mom shared one of those secret smiles with Ebonee that always made Talia bristle imagining what they said about her.

She unwound her scarf and headed to the coat closet. She'd taken their snide remarks to her face all of her life. Back in the kitchen, she strode to her mother's side and pressured her shoulder until she faced Talia. "Mom, I've always wondered about something. Did you love Ebonee's father more than mine? Is that why she's always been the apple of your eye and I grew up an unwanted heavyweight appendage?"

Mom scowled, sputtered, and retreated until the pantry door ended her escape.

"You've favored your firstborn all my life, though I'm guessing Ebonee weighs more than I do right now."

Her sister sucked in a loud gasp, crossed her arms, and leaned against the stainless steel refrigerator. If the glare she shot at Talia were a bullet, she'd be slammed to the floor.

Tears blossomed in Mom's hazel eyes. Her lower lip trembled. She drew in a long breath and covered Talia's hand. "It was never about you, my girl. Except for the genes she got from her father that colored her skin, Ebonee reinforced my own appearance. That's all I had in life, was my looks. You came along and brought out all my insecurities."

Waterworks now rained down Mom's cheeks, transforming mascara, blush, and foundation into a muddy rivulet.

Talia inhaled and exhaled, captured her upper lip with her teeth to keep from interrupting.

Mom grabbed a piece of paper towel and blew her nose. She smiled through her sniffles. "You were smarter at two years old than anyone I'd ever met. You honestly intimidated me by the time you went to kindergarten. You still do by that job at the hospital I don't understand, and your work at the church. But I love you as much as I'm able. And I'm prouder of you than I can put into words. You are now as beautiful on the outside as you've ever been on the inside. I've just never been able to tell you."

"But why has it been easier for you say mean things all my life?" Talia glanced over Mom's shoulder as Ebonee came up to put an arm around both of them.

Mom shrugged her shoulders and leaned her head on Talia. A moment later, Mom raised her arms and the three huddled in a bond of tears and love that was brand spankin' new to Talia. Her mother's embrace melted years of hurt. A Christmas miracle.

Ebonee finally broke away and blew her nose. "Little sister, please forgive me. Momma has always been my whole world and the example I've followed forever. But I think I'm ready to visit this new church you're attending now and see if I can become a better person."

"That makes two of us, girls. I've never gone to church on a Sunday morning. And that's another way you've made me feel inferior, Talia. You took yourself off to church starting at age thirteen. I never understood where that desire came about. And now it's a habit."

Talia's heart pumped hard and fast. "From reading. I wanted to check out what I'd seen and heard on TV. I found Jesus that way, and I've read the Bible ever since."

"Okay, before you leave today, we'll decide where to meet you come Sunday. Ebonee, you're picking me up."

"You'll never know how wonderful those words sound." Talia's heart now raced for another reason. "I'll introduce you to a man who has changed my outlook lately. It'll be fun to see if you remember me talking about him."

For the first time she could recall, the Ashby women shared a pleasant meal. Mom had stopped herself more than a couple times from speaking. It proved she had taken the time to think first, and then changed her mind about whatever she bit back from saying.

During the meal Ebonee told several stories about the factory where she worked and their holiday rush on the assembly lines. Presents were exchanged without derogatory comments. Ebonee also brought two new word games and they'd spent a good afternoon actually enjoying one another's company.

What an affirmation to never give up hope. She'd pray every spare minute until Sunday that Mom and Ebonee would actually show up for church service. What would they think of meeting the pastor who'd come to Talia's rescue years ago?

Though Ebonee had been loaded down with fudge and cookies, Talia took home her leftover salad, hardly touched, and plain sweet potatoes. She didn't mind because she also carried away a baggie with turkey scraps for Cookie.

She texted Cooper that she didn't mind how late he called. She stayed up, listened to Christmas music, and sipped spiced cider, staring at the Christmas tree until Cooper called at ten minutes past midnight.

"Hey, my dazzling beauty, how was your day?"

"Close to miraculous. Imagine yours was rowdy."

"That it was. Kids and wrapping paper and food and noise."

"It sounds like lots of love to me. I didn't have the tension filled time we're in the habit of creating."

"Do tell. You were already anxious the night before."

Talia told him all about what transpired that day.

"Sounds like my prayers worked. And God worked. I've only been here two days and I miss you. I so wish you would have changed your mind and come with me."

"As I said earlier, Cooper, I would have felt out of place since we're not actually dating. Maybe I can meet just your parents and be introduced as a good friend."

"When is it going to sink in that you're more than a friend? Even the boys in youth group see how I feel about you."

"What? You haven't told them we're an item, or dating, have you?"

"They're guys, no matter their young age. I can't help it if I look at you with love in my eyes."

How should she respond to that? Her gaze landed on the unwrapped gift beneath her tree. She'd found a wooden model of Cooper's canary yellow sports car that she visualized as a unique birdhouse.

"Talia? You still there?"

"I zoned out staring at your Christmas present under my tree. And realize how tired I am. Is it all right if we say good night?"

"Not really, sleeping beauty, but we'll talk tomorrow. And then the thirtieth will be here before you know it. I'll bring over your present then."

Her stomach growled. Should she go to bed hungry, or follow the urge to gorge herself? The noise from her gut reinforced that the more you ate the more you wanted to eat. *Change your thoughts, ignore the temptation.*

An image of Cooper shot into her head. It would prove a wasted attempt to rid herself of loving the man. Why was she unwilling to follow her heart and give in to what she knew soul deep? The fear of saddling him with another woman who battled eating issues, who would disappoint him by what she saw in the mirror, made a mockery of all her efforts to help the junior high girls.

✝✝✝

The five days following Christmas crawled for Talia. But the world had sped up as soon as Cooper returned on the thirtieth and invited her on a New Year's Eve date. So here they were, on their way to spend the day with Pastor Kendall and June Rose.

Pastor greeted them at the door. "Happy almost New Year. June Rose is in the kitchen and assures me we will eat shortly." He took their coats, hung them in the hall closet, and threw an arm over Cooper's shoulders.

Talia followed her nose to the wonderful aroma of buttery seafood. "Hey, June Rose, it smells delicious."

"Hi, yourself. Oyster stew and potato soup are the perfect temp so we'll eat before the milk scalds." A stack of plates rested near a cold cut platter and decorative crackers on the dividing island.

"What can I do to help?"

"There's a pitcher of lemon water in the fridge if you wouldn't mind filling the glasses."

"I'd be happy to." Talia glanced at the diminutive woman as she turned off a burner. "June Rose, as a young girl were you teased about your size?"

"Merciful heavens yes. My father and uncles were the worst. Pip-squeak, midget, baby, kid, freak. You name it."

"Did it bother you?" Talia poured the fragrant water into a second poinsettia painted glass. "I'm asking because I grew up heavy. As a girl, I'd have made more than two of you. Even my mom said my waist was larger than hers at age ten."

"I'm sorry you had to go through that, but look at you now!" June Rose accepted the near-empty pitcher and set it on the counter. "Don't you think every woman who's gone through teen years has issues about her physical appearance?"

"Unfortunately. And I think it's a shame. A Bible study topic for sure."

Cooper and Kendall walked in, still yakking football. Kendall grabbed a celery stalk and scooped up a glob of spinach-artichoke dip. "This goop is so good. Since you and Cooper deal with teens, I'd like to express my feelings about women."

"Women?" June Rose swatted his hand as Kendall reached for a green-frosted gingerbread cookie. "I thought I was the only woman you knew about."

"I'll never claim to know about you, my love. You remain a mystery in many ways, much the way King Solomon expressed. The wisest man in the world couldn't fathom the way of a man with a maid."

Cooper leaned his shoulder against the stainless steel refrigerator. Talia hid her grin as his cheeks turned a pale shade of pink. "Women are a dichotomy."

"That they are. But so lovable." Kendall danced away from June Rose's swat. "Soft yet strong."

She reached for Kendall's hand.

He glanced at Talia, then Cooper. "Have you ever heard the joke about Eve trying on different tree leaves for size? She asked Adam which one made her look the best."

"Oh, you." June Rose blushed prettily and removed her apron.

Kendall pulled her into his side. "Gentle yet firm. Kind yet tough."

"Smarter. Deeper." Cooper joined in.

"From what I've observed…" Kendall kissed the top of his wife's silver hair. "Their capacity to love is a thousand times greater than men's."

"They smile when they should scream." Cooper nudged Talia's foot.

She turned her head with expectation for Kendall's next comment.

"Sing rather than cry." He didn't disappoint, and the tennis match was on between the two men.

"Cry when they want to use their fists."

"Fight to be heard." Cooper kept his gaze fixed on Talia.

"Listen with their hearts."

June Rose snuggled up to her husband over that one.

"Cover humiliation with pride."

"Use wisdom to figure out things rather than jump in to fix whatever's wrong."

Talia straightened and held out her hands in the stop gesture. "You two make us girls sound perfect when we are the opposite."

Cooper shrugged and slanted a perplexed look at Kendall. "Why don't they see their worth?"

Kendall laughed. "That's the question for the ages. Especially with Christ, a woman's heart should be happily satisfied at all times. My woman satisfies my stomach at all times. Let's eat."

Hours later, Talia awakened from a bad dream…*I don't want her. You can have her. She's too fat for me.* She battled the taunting tune the rest of the sleepless night. She'd never live up to the accolades the two pastors had bounced back and forth.

Chapter 12

JANUARY PASSED IN A DRAG of cloudy days and snowed-in weekends. Six weeks into the new year, it was now the Saturday before Valentine's Day and Talia welcomed nine girls into her home. Shannon's mother had apologized for her accusations against Talia and the girl had bounced back with health on her mind rather than pounds shown on a scale.

Cookie was out of control over all the attention and noise the girls ushered inside. She lolled her tongue, rolled over and exposed her belly, leaped and ran in circles.

"She's happy, Miss Talia. I think I love her." Janiyah knelt and hugged the pup.

The girls fired questions about the dog.

"What is she?"

Talia loved the attention as much as her pup. "Goldendoodles are a fairly new dog breed around twenty years old. They're considered a designer breed because each of their parents is a purebred, a poodle and golden retriever. Cookie's father is a standard poodle. That's why she has such long legs."

"Her pretty, curly hair is so soft. Does it get all over your house?"

"Poodles don't shed. They're athletic and intelligent, Goldendoodles are also lovable, family dogs full of playful energy. I chose Cookie because she approached me in the kennel and will be my forever friend. She enjoys running so that helps me keep in shape by walking with her.”

“How big will she get?”

“Goldendoodles weigh between fifty and a hundred pounds. I’m thinking Cookie will be seventy to seventy-five.”

“Does she play catch or fetch?”

“Yes. She loves Frisbee and anyone who will play with her in the backyard.”

“I’m glad you have such a good friend.”

“Great friend, but not so good at being a guard dog. If you noticed, she didn’t even bark when you knocked at the door.”

“That’s okay, girl.” Aleah sunk her face against Cookie’s ruff. “Not a thing wrong with being calm and friendly.”

“May I give her a treat?”

“Maybe later.” Talia stood with a laugh. “That’s enough about Cookie. We’re here to mix up no-bake healthy treats. Sasha and Aleah, could you please gather jackets and pile them on the guest bed around the corner to the left?”

Lydia slid on the floor in her stocking feet into a prone position. “Come here, sweet Cookie. I could go nuts loving on you. Who needs my help making nutritious energy bites?”

Talia adored all the attention shown to her dog. “Cookie will need replenished when this day is over.”

“How old is she?”

Talia answered without determining who had asked. “She turns one on Valentine’s Day, which is my birthday too.”

“That’s tomorrow! Do you make her good treats, Miss Talia?”

Cookie sat at the word treat.

"I've thought about it, but since she's still a puppy, I get her appropriate goodies from the pet store." Talia held back the pup as Lydia stood. Would she be all right or should Talia crate her? She'd never been around so many people, especially inside.

"Do you feed her people food?"

"Rarely, and then only bits of meat." Talia stood. "Stay down, girl. The rest of us will be busy." They all remained close to the entry. "First things first. Three of you at each sink. One between the bedrooms, one through my room, and here in the kitchen. Then we'll get started."

She ran a practiced eye over ingredients lined up across the kitchen counters. Butter, dark cocoa, mini marshmallows, and raw sugar next to the stove. Vanilla, almond, butter flavoring along with honey and maple syrup for liquids. Peanut butter in small jars, more softened butter, and three sets of measuring utensils.

By that time, all the girls lined up on the living room side of the chest-high island. "In front of you are three sets of mixing stuff and a choice of three recipes. I'd like you to remain in the groups the way you washed up. Decide on which recipe you'd like to make. One of the three requires stirring a pot on the stove. The other two use the raw ingredients I've set out."

She gave them time to decide while she checked the cartons of old-fashioned oats and the unsweetened coconut flakes. She gave the pink sea salt a shake. "You have options for the recipe that only calls for oats. I often add hulled sunflower seeds, flax seeds, or pumpkin seeds. If you do, remember to adjust the amount of oats. Same goes for the variety of chocolate, butterscotch, or white chips."

"These really look good, Miss Talia." Shannon hesitated. "Is it good to eat so much fat though?"

"The butter and peanut butter are organic. A balanced diet includes healthy fats with each meal. These recipes won't hurt you unless you eat a whole pan." She smiled at the chorus of giggles, yucks, and yums.

The group that had washed at the kitchen sink opted for the cooking recipe that included raw sugar and cocoa. They gathered around the stove. The other two each chose different recipes.

"If you have any questions at all concerning measurements or substitutions, please ask. But I can only speak to one of you at a time."

"I've never seen or heard of chia seeds," Sasha commented.

"I'm always suggesting you discover things for yourselves by researching. Chia seeds are an ancient grain that's become popular used in smoothies and nutritional baking in recent years." Talia said a silent thank you to herself for not setting out hemp seeds. She probably could have without naming them, but didn't want to get into a discussion about them not being a derivative of marijuana.

"My aunt says flax is better ground up for nutritional value." Aleah held a questioning glint in her bright blue eyes, so Talia answered.

"She's right. And I do have ground flax in the pantry if you prefer. The other seeds help these bars contain enough nutrition."

Shannon spit into her hand. "I tasted the coconut. Yuck."

Talia softly laughed. "Wash that hand, please. In fact, all of you wipe your hands often as you're mixing and measuring and stirring. Here's your chance to use math skills. There are enough goods to make double recipes, so I expect you to talk to each other and get it done. Any more questions?"

It did her heart good to stand aside and let the girls do their thing. Once eighth grade was over for the two oldest, would she ever have contact with them again? For that matter, would the others return to youth group the next school year?

"Miss Talia." Janiyah turned. "I think we've stirred this enough. What pan do we put this mix in?"

Talia led them to the table. "I have small aluminum pans so each of you can take home a share of what you've made. Please line the pans with wax paper. You'll see I have extra pans. I thought it would be nice for each group to set samples aside for Pastor Cooper and the boys. I can bring them on Wednesday."

"I love that idea." Shannon bounced on the balls of her feet. Her facial color was good and she no longer seemed gaunt. Two of the other girls had grown two-three inches, so she didn't appear as out of place as she had at the beginning of the year.

"They last that long?" Lydia asked with a frown.

"In the fridge they do. Up to two weeks." While the girls shaped balls and patted ingredients into the pans, Talia mixed up a concoction—that word immediately placed a picture in her head of Cooper grinning over his sweet cherry drink—of yummy flavored bites. "Wash really well once finished, and then we can have a treat while the goodies cool. I have milk or water. Glasses on the shelf with the open cupboard door. Help yourselves."

Cookie chose that moment to wake from her nap and wrapped Talia's waist in a hug of long furry legs. She kissed the pup on the head. "You are such a good girl. I have a special duck treat for you, one you haven't had yet."

The dog sat without being told, and smiled the whole time Talia sought the treat from the pantry. Cookie gobbled it up and went begging to each girl where they stood around the table laughing and tasting.

Talia soaked in the giggles and the girly noise. She'd never thought much about having children of her own, probably due to her unpleasant childhood memories. Would she be happier if she'd been attractive, thin, and lovable the way Ebonee had always been? What about Cooper? He'd never said if he thought about becoming a father. Maybe not, since he claimed he was an over-grown kid himself.

"Miss Talia?"

The sound of her name jerked her from her thoughts. "Yes, Aleah?"

"Your place is nice. Do you have a good job? And did you have to go to college for it?"

"I'm a data research analysist for hospitals and have an office in the largest hospital in the city. I did go to college and have a degree."

"Didja ever work anywhere else?"

"Yes, Janiyah. I used to attend the largest church in Lincoln. I worked in their bookstore while I went to school."

As often happens, there was a lull in conversation as tins were covered and sorted.

Sasha finished first and dived into her phone. "Oh wow. Catch what I've just found." Girls gathered around to look at the phone.

"That's a cross." Janiyah pointed.

"Laminin. 'A molecular weight, a protein network

foundation for most cells and organs.'"

"Shaped like a cross." Aleah locked eyes with Talia. "God put a tiny, tiny life-giving thing in our bodies shaped like a cross."

Talia tapped it in on her own phone. Did Cooper know about this? "Now that's awesome. God's totally beyond words. He's so amazing."

She again stood back, watching and listening. *Lord God, thank You for these girls. Draw me to You closer than I've ever been. Help me be who You want me to be.*

Before long it was time to wrap up their day. "Girls, if you haven't texted or called your rides, please do that now. Don't forget your healthy energy treats."

Lydia and Sasha lingered, though an older sister climbed out of her car at the curb. "We've never been to The South Four for smoothies and would like to talk to you. Could you meet us there tomorrow right after church?"

Talia had no plans, but she checked her phone calendar so the girls didn't think her social life pathetic. She nodded. "See you then."

Too bad one of those energetic souls couldn't have stayed to walk the dog. Leash in hand, she slipped on her jacket and shoes. "All right, Lord, please make it a good reason for the meeting and not that another girl is in trouble. Without Cooper's close support as with Janiyah and Shannon, I don't think I could deal with any of their problems on my own."

Chapter 13

COOPER SAT ALONE AT A table in South Four Java and Juice, trying to figure out which kid had what kind of problem. Was it wrong to think there'd be trouble-free days until school let out in the spring? Talia hadn't mentioned that any of the girls were hurting. In fact, after Sunday school he'd heard the giggling tribe chatter about how much fun they'd had cooking at Talia's place yesterday. Just as he thought of her, there she stood inside the door scanning the room.

She jutted her chin and strode his way. "Someone must really be in trouble if they asked us both here."

He used his foot to slide out a chair for her, and then stood to pull it from the table. He tracked the parking lot and saw none of the kids. "Lydia and Shannon asked me to come here. I guess I should read the note they handed me after Sunday school."

"I'll get a drink. Carmel macchiato for me today."

He unfolded the paper. Burst into laughter over what he read. *Talia's birthday is today. February 14th. Valentine's Day*. It was signed *YOLO*.

She swung from the counter and caught his gaze as if agreeing that you only live once on this earth. And he longed to spend time with her. As she neared with her drink, one smooth move removed her jacket.

They both checked the parking lot through the window. Talia piled her jacket on top of her purse that sat on the empty chair. "Did I hear you laughing?"

"Yep. Our secret is out, my sweet Talia."

She frowned and tested the heat of her drink. "What do you mean?"

He tapped his fingers on the folded note. "I have a feeling we've been set up."

"What's on the paper?"

Cooper sat forward, battling the grin that wanted to spread. He used both hands to unfold the note, smoothed the plain white paper, and then turned it so she could read it. Oh, to know what ran through her head. He sure got a kick out of the expressions that washed across her face. Curiosity. Puzzlement. Realization.

"Me and my big mouth." Her forehead creased. "What's YOLO?"

"You Only Live Once. Happy Birthday. Now I know what I saw the girls hand you this morning. Care to elaborate on the big mouth?"

She met his gaze. Shook her head and laughed, jostling her shoulders forward. "Cookie's birthday is the same as mine. I told the girls when they were at my house yesterday, and they gave me cards today."

He traced the fingers of her free hand at a snail's pace. Such soft skin over the delicate blue veins, a little rough around the cuticles due to the weather, then the unblemished texture of the nails. From her thumb, he turned up her hand and drew lazy hearts in the palm. He could touch her all afternoon.

She tried to pull back, but he held on.

"Those kids have a fine idea. The two of us, together. Do you want to give us a try, get to know each other better than friends? I see so much when I look at you. One of those things is stated in II Corinthians 2:15. You, my sweet Talia, are the pleasing aroma of Christ among those who are being saved and those who are perishing. You mean the world to those girls. They love you." *As do I.*

She sighed, nudged her hand forward, and linked their fingers. "I've missed our times together. Now you know my birthday. When's yours?"

Maybe someday he'd confess how she'd left a hole in his life at the word chill, as in cooling their time spent together. Right now, he was plenty warm. "We're four months apart to the day. October fourteenth. And before you ask, I was born in Kansas."

"If we count the other way, we're eight months apart. We graduated together. Which is oldest?"

"Do you analyze everything? It doesn't matter to me."

Her soft laughter whispered down his spine.

"By the way…" He squeezed her hand. "I approve of the scarf. Don't black and white get boring after a while?"

She picked up one end of the scarf and ran the tassels over his nose. "Red is for Valentine's Day. I learned a long time ago that black is classy. I dress up because it makes me feel good."

"I think there's more to it." He didn't allow his gaze to waver from hers.

"You should have been a psychologist. Since I've worked through this, there is. I see the world as black and white. Don't believe in gray. Maybe gray describes my parents. They never married. Dad wasn't in the picture much. When he was, I didn't tell him Mom constantly compared me to my older sister, Ebonee. I guess I did have one up on her. She never knew her father." Talia shrugged. "I set high self-standards and try my darnedest to live up to them. If I say I'm right, I'm right."

Wow. She had a similar background to many of the junior high kids. No wonder God hand-picked her to work with them. He fought for breath as he studied her lips work around the lid of the paper cup to get all the creamy froth.

She raised her eyelids and caught him. One corner of her mouth quirked upward. "Since we're on this getting-to-know-you date." Her eyes rounded. "Is this a date?"

"Those girls set us up. So, yes, I suppose it is."

Her face blanked but she couldn't cover up the sparkle in her eyes. "So, Pastor Cooper Valiant, what do you do in your spare time besides build birdhouses?"

"I'm enthralled by the stories of missionary martyrs. Our news doesn't talk about those brave, God-chosen warriors who give their lives for the sake of the Gospel. David Livingstone was a Scottish doctor who explored Africa in the nineteenth century. There are countless others. You should look them up sometime. The numbers of those Christians, the most martyred of all religions, will astound you. How about you? What do you do when you're not working?"

Her laugh washed over him like the sunshine on this February day. Did she remember how often they advised the kids to check out questions for themselves? "The lives of missionaries sound fascinating. I told you I'm boring. As for me, I read about nutrition and follow weight loss blogs."

He mimed gagging. "Not really. You keep in shape that way. And I would be the last person on earth to call you boring."

She heaved a sigh and pulled her hand from his grasp. "Our drinks are gone. What do we do next?"

"Walk with me?"

They nestled into coat collars and donned gloves.

He offered his elbow as the door shut behind them, and she snuggled against his side.

After a moment, she laughed.

"What's so funny?"

"I haven't trudged along this slow since my thighs rubbed together and I had no energy to go faster. So sorry, Cooper. Too much information."

"That doesn't sound humorous to me. Tell me something I don't know about you."

"Hmm. Did you know I never knew anything about my dad's life? He disappeared when I was eleven. Just stopped coming around. My mom's name is Donna and we still have a few issues. It's hard for me to get over the ways of our dysfunctional relationship."

"Are you and Ebonee alike?"

"Not at all. She was always perfect. Hair, skin, body. And Mom let me know it. We're civil but I'll never be close to her the way I am to Heather, a friend whom I work with."

"I'm sorry you had to deal with all of that growing up. It was hard enough at school for you, but to deal with put-downs at home had to be incredibly hard." He drew to a stop at the curb for a car turning the corner. "Who are your other friends?"

"I kept in touch with a couple gals from college for a little while, but I'd say the guy in the next office at work, David, is a good friend." She stepped into the street.

"Should I be jealous?"

She jabbed him with her elbow. "Silly boy. He's married and has three kids. I connect with Janiyah. I hope we can be friends as she goes through school."

"That would be nice." He dropped his chin into his

jacket collar. "Does it feel colder to you? Let's turn around and get going."

"Sounds good to me." She let go of his arm and switched to walk on his other side. She allowed him to protect her from the traffic. He liked that.

Later at her car door, he took her hands and swung their arms out to the sides. "The last time I stood on your stoop you said something about a crush putting the brakes on our time together. Did you crush on me, Talia?"

"It was my secret for years. I had a mad crush on you. You've always been friendly, extroverted, and nosy. A bit wacky and kid-like. Now that I've seen you with the young teens, you melt my heart over how much you care for others in general. I'm conflicted because for some reason I thought it was wrong for us to spend time together. That it's not a good example for the kids and others to see us, but—"

He held up his hand in a stop-sign motion. "It's not about other people. Being with you tonight was great. The best Valentine's Day I've ever had. I'm so sorry I didn't know it was your birthday. I'll surprise you some other time."

"Let's take it slow and see where the Lord leads us."

"Does that mean I can ask you for another date? The football game was first."

At her nod, he released her hands and pulled her into a hug. After all day long, he drew in her signature fragrance of tangy grapefruit and a hint of the patchouli. He'd always associate those scents with her. He whispered against her ear, "I'm holding back with everything I have. I'd love to give you a sound birthday kiss right now, but I'm saving it for a surprise."

✞✞✞

The following Wednesday night, Talia hid a smile as she observed Cooper rein in his energy as he paced in between greeting the youth. Whenever he let loose his excitement, he bounced around rowdier than the teens. Once they were all seated, he began.

"Tonight's lesson is on godly living. Anyone want to say what that means?"

"Do what's right. Don't get in with a wrong crowd."

"Take out the trash and watch the back talk."

"Don't steal or make fun of others."

Cooper paced the front of the room. "How do we stick to the right behavior?"

"Come here and go to Sunday school."

She was pleased with the offering of answers, so much different from their reticence at the beginning of the school year.

"Now we're getting to the root of our help." Cooper stopped to face the kids, though he swayed from one foot to the other. "We need to hear the Word of God for right living to take place. Hearing is one of our senses. Listening uses common sense. Putting knowledge into action takes wisdom. How does God's Word sink in?"

"Read it, study it, memorize."

"Attend worship and SS, hang out with good kids."

"Ah. The company we keep is huge. There's a verse for that in the Bible. Anyone know where?"

The response was downcast eyes and twitchy movements.

"Let's turn to I Corinthians 15:33. We'll read it together."

Talia pulled out her Bible, which she preferred over technology.

Cooper began reading and the students mumbled along. "'Do not be misled: Bad company corrupts good character.' Burke mentioned memorizing Scripture. I'd like you all to memorize this one."

Janiyah caught Talia's attention and they shared a smile.

Cooper went on. "I remember reading the Bible at your age and wondering why we had to know certain things. Scripture has a purpose for us throughout our lives. As you read and study and put right things into practice, you'll find how those words speak to you at the times you need them, wherever you are at that moment in your lives. You'll learn. There's even a verse in II Corinthians that tells us not to marry unbelievers."

He paced twice, and then turned to her. "Miss Talia, anything you'd like to add?"

She stood and faced the chairs. "It's easy to not always understand the Bible. But we have a responsibility as Christians to accept it. We do that by our faith. We should acknowledge the Bible as God's truth. I know it's hard. My mother taught me right from wrong, but in today's world, those lines become more blurred every day. Some people say we live in a gray world. The Bible is the only example of what's right and what's wrong."

"Thank you." Cooper took over. "There's a verse I want you all to write down. Read it on your own later. Be sure you mark it and know where it is. I Corinthians 6:18."

Talia spoke up. "May I add I Corinthians 10:13?"

"Definitely. Thank you." Cooper's infectious smile could be Talia's undoing. He continued. "My parents knew black and white. They taught right and wrong. Our teachers and politicians of today don't live by those principles. And that's a whole area I'm not getting into. We've had a heavy discussion tonight. Let's play some death ball. Circle the chairs, everyone."

Talia and Cooper both counted to make sure the circle of chairs was one less than players. Cooper stood in the middle and called up one of the boys. He explained if the beach ball touched a seated player somewhere other than hands, that person went to the middle. If the passed ball hit a body or the person in the middle, a chase ensued.

Contagious laughter took Talia by surprise. She couldn't help but join the fray. Those kids were nuts, especially the boys. Cooper gave them twenty minutes and then called a halt for the youth to divide into their sessions.

The girls were all smiles as Talia turned things serious in their circle following the game.

"Are you all clear on living by the Word?"

Lydia spoke up. "I get it, but it's not easy."

"How do we live that way, Miss Talia?"

"Thanks for asking, Janiyah. We obey what God says as He convicts us. Most of those commands are in the New Testament. But loving Him with all our heart, mind, and soul comes from Deuteronomy."

Aleah raised her hand. "What does that mean?"

"The first thing, of course, is to acknowledge our sin and need for Jesus in our lives. Then again, every time we're in trouble, or feeling good about life, think about God first. By seeing Him, or Jesus, in our minds, we take the focus off ourselves and this world."

"Living as a Christian isn't easy." Shannon slumped in her seat.

"You're right. I admit it doesn't get easier. Loving God that much, with everything that we are, is tough because we're selfish. But we get strength from God. As we put Him first, our lives allow others to see Christ in us because we want to please Him. Once school is out for summer, I suggest you read books by trusted Christian authors. I'll help you any time you want. That's a long way off. Now, let's turn to Zephaniah 3:17. 'The LORD your God is with you, the Mighty Warrior who saves. He will take great delight in you; in his love he will no longer rebuke you, but will rejoice over you with singing.'"

"Sometimes the Old Testament is hard to read. I like that verse." Aleah closed her Bible and ran a tender hand over the cover.

"What do you want? Figure it out. Pray, and go for it unless you hit a stop sign." She waited a beat. The girls remained quiet. "I'd like to share my favorite verses with you. Psalm 139:13-14 says, 'For You created my inmost being; You knit me together in my mother's womb. I praise You because I am fearfully and wonderfully made; Your works are wonderful, I know that full well.' I hope you read it often."

No one commented that they'd read it together before. She prayed they'd remember and it would soon become ingrained.

"Let's have brownies and call it a night."

A half hour later, a blast of frigid air hit Talia as Cooper held the church door open. A moist Canadian front had descended with icy wind gusts. She huddled next to his side. "Brr. The forecasters were right."

Cooper leaned in with his arm around her back and they took off running. The damp cold penetrated through her clothing and drove straight to the bone.

Fern frost covered the Jeep windows. "It's so pretty, I don't want to scrape it off.

Cooper hadn't said a word, but leaned in close at her Jeep door. "You'll never see that belated birthday connection coming."

What? Her nerve endings came to life over the imagined thrill of his kiss. She was ready to pledge her love for him, heart, body, and soul. Wouldn't he be surprised if she turned her cheek just a tad and allowed her lips to kiss his first?

Chapter 14

THE THIRD SATURDAY OF MARCH presented a clear blue sky with a little breeze and hints of spring sunshine. Talia pinned cobalt blue ribbons that represented the Eating Disorder Awareness Walk on the shirts of five girls from youth group. She'd sponsored two girls and the parents of the other three registered them.

"This is great, Miss Talia. No more FoMo for me. Thanks for asking us to come with you." Shannon smiled wide and waved her arms.

Would she ever understand their language? "What's FoMo mean again?"

Janiyah answered. "Fear of missing out. Me either. I didn't want to hear how much fun you all had and later wished I'd of come."

"Makes sense. I wonder if Pastor Cooper knows what FoMo means. I'm proud of you for walking with me. Thank the Lord for such a mild day. We should be invigorated when finished rather than exhausted."

"Yeah. I was tuckered out after cooking in your kitchen."

The other girls razzed Aleah, but it was all in fun. Cooking just wasn't her thing.

"Next time we get together outside Wednesday night it'll be cooking in the church kitchen. We'll sell the results to the congregation to help with camp costs."

"Good way to make bucks," Aleah spoke up again. "I

want to invite a friend to camp. Would people go for those healthy protein bites if we sell them?"

Talia gave Aleah a fist bump. "I had planned on making several energy bites. Fudge or brownies are good too. Bring your recipes the next time we're together and if there's a problem cooking at home, let me know. As for friends, of course they are welcome."

The group of close to two thousand walkers grew silent as a handful of people took a makeshift stage. Fulfillment washed through Talia. The girls listened as if spellbound while two young women presented testimonies from opposite sides of eating disorders dilemma. *Thank You, Lord, for repurposing my life. It's been an honor to spend time with these girls. I hope and pray You want me to continue this work You've called me to.*

The spokesperson thanked participants for taking part in the walk, gave encouragement for keeping up with a healthy lifestyle, and then instructed them how to line up for the five-mile walk through southeast Lincoln.

Talia would rather be running, but by moving slow, she could converse with the girls.

"Will the money we earn from baked stuff be enough to help us get to camp?" Lydia swiped at her forehead and walked backward as she waited for an answer. "Couldn't we, like, bring plants or books to sell along with the healthy goodies we make?"

"Great idea." Aleah flipped her ponytail. "Then I wouldn't have to make a mess in any kitchen."

Talia gauged the other girls' expressions. "I'll check with Pastor Cooper. I see no reason for him not to agree for us girls to expand the sale a bit. Camp costs are a good cause."

Sasha swung in a circle. "I think it's a terrific idea."

"The guys will say it's better than workin' to earn bucks."

Janiyah snapped her fingers. "More cheddar fo' us."

That drew a laugh from more than Talia's team. Cheddar obviously meant money.

Silence fell over the group of six, which gave her the chance to breathe in the smell of the great outdoors. Damp earth, the tree skeletons that held that greenish fuzz that indicated they'd soon burst forth in the splendor of the leaves God dressed them in. She'd grown used to telling herself every day that she needed to get over the fat issue of her youth and accept herself as God's unique creation. He'd gone so far as to adopt her as His daughter.

In other words, to coin a cliché, practice what she preached to the teenagers.

She again ran an eye over her companions. These girls on the brink of womanhood had become her mission, her passion. She wanted none of them to regret having an eating disorder or carry a body image that prevented them from experiencing a healthy relationship with a boy or young man. Talia opened her listening heart to the conversations going on around her.

Janiyah. "It wasn't easy getting over the anxiety I had about my outside appearance. Focusing on myself is not the way to fit in with others or make new friends."

Shannon. "I had to figure out I wasn't on public display, though I felt that way. I wanted acceptance rather than rejection. I fit in because, thanks to Miss Talia and Pastor Coop, I know I'm loved by the Lord."

Talia couldn't keep quiet. "I once thought that others, my mom, sister, and boys in particular, wanted to see perfection rather than flaws. I don't believe that now. Pastor Cooper has actually helped me understand on a deeper level that every person is God's individualized creation. Getting to know others, having true friends, means we take off our masks and bare our souls so people see us the way we are."

Lydia. "I get what all of you are saying, but I think I've always accepted myself as the way God made me."

Talia caught a hint of pride in the statement but didn't want to point it out in front of the other girls.

Aleah. "We're saved by grace. Fearfully and wonderfully made."

Talia stopped to hug every single one. Other walkers parted to move around them. "It does my heart good to know that you've opened your hearts and listened."

"Yes. God's Love Makes All The Difference." Sasha jostled two steps ahead and walked sideways. "Miss Talia, I've wondered ever since you told us your story, did being heavy for so long harm your body?"

Talia faced her, taking side steps also. "I've been blessed by genetics to have excellent blood work. My cholesterol numbers and blood pressure have always been good, which isn't the MO of most overweight people." *Now who sounded prideful?* She turned her head and studied the other girls' faces. "As I've come to know you all, helped you accept yourselves despite my own fears of gaining too much weight someday, I've come to understand my wounds of obesity don't have to scar or label me. I have a sense of love and belonging I never knew before this past school year."

The girls did some kind of eye connect and broke into a rap rhythm to the accompaniment of Janiyah's sound effects. "Wednesday night treats turned into Wednesday night meets. Talia and Pastor Coop are in a love loop."

Talia's cheeks heated and she slowed to walk a step behind the girls.

✝✝✝

Later in the shower ridding herself of the results from her sweaty walk with Cookie, she replayed conversation with the girls. Ever since the girls sang their ditty, *Wednesday night treats turned into Wednesday night meets. Talia and Pastor Coop are in a love loop*, thoughts of Cooper had filled her soul. Emotions as furious as ocean breakers crashing against rocky cliffs beat against the walls of Talia's being.

He had yet to surprise her with the kiss he'd promised on Valentine's Day, and she'd been antsy with anticipation every time they were alone. They often sat together for worship and met at Aleah's family's South Four for drinks, gone on movie dates, or driven around the countryside surrounding the city. By now all the youth and close congregants treated them as a couple.

Cooper on her mind gave way to the girls. She couldn't be more pleased with their attitudes, their selflessness, and the growing friendships that had blossomed. One of the girls had the idea of passing around their journals so they could sign each other's on the inside cover. Another suggested they pray for one another during the summer. Janiyah wanted to know if they could get together after school let out, maybe once in July and again in August.

A knock sounded on Talia's door as she left her room.

Through the window, she spied Cooper. Those ocean waves took up their thrashing beat in her heart.

Cookie ran and slid across the floor.

"Sit, girl." Talia opened the door, leaned her temple

against the edge. The man before her made her dizzy with the driving waves that thumped inside her chest wall.

"Hey, love. I couldn't wait until tomorrow morning to see you at church. I thought of going for a walk but after what you did today, can we sit outside and talk?" He slid her a shy smile, uncharacteristic of the bouncy guy.

"Sounds great." She opened the door and Cookie thudded her paws against Cooper's chest.

He removed her feet and walked the pup backward.

"I was about to have some fruit flavored sparkling water. Cranberry or orange for you?"

"Orange, please. Come on dog, let's play out back." Cookie followed at his heel and raced by Cooper as soon as the slider gave her enough room. "Nice patio. Bet you're thankful for the roof come late summer."

"Thanks. I'll be right out." She set the tall glasses of flavored water and ginger ale on the glass-topped table and leaned over the rail. Would the man always have as much energy as a kid? Cookie was in dog heaven over a rousing game of fetch, but after ten minutes, plopped on her side with the chew rope extending from both sides of her mouth.

Cooper bounded to the patio and guzzled half his drink.

Taking in his actions, followed by a swipe of his brow and face-splitting grin, Talia grew lightheaded all over again. What was wrong with her?

He ran a finger up her arm as he sat next to her.

The thin sleeve of her athletic top might just as well have been nonexistent. Her hand shook as she reached for her glass, so she let it alone.

He folded her hand in his, played with the fingers one by one in his signature movement, along with drawing hearts in her palm.

She laid her head back against the lounge chair and closed her eyes. *Wednesday night treats turned into Wednesday night meets. Talia and Pastor Coop are in a love loop.*

"How many girls showed up for the walking disorder event today?"

"Five. Those girls are something else, Cooper. Is it wrong to be proud of them, as though I had something to do with their changes?" Should she share their matchmaking ditty?

"Be proud in what the Lord has done. As I'm proud of you." He crossed an ankle over a knee and jiggled his foot. "You've been forthright with me, I want to get it all out, bare my soul to you about something that's bothered me for a long time. I've prayed about it and believe as close as we've grown, that by sharing how awful I was to my sister, maybe I can finally put it behind me."

She threaded their fingers and squeezed twice. "You really have a secret of misbehavior? Guess I'll have to take you off that pedestal."

"Don't joke, Talia. No way should I be on a pedestal. I was so ashamed of the way Analise looked that I avoided her at a shopping mall. She waved from a carousel, but I was with my friends and ignored her."

"You were probably as embarrassed as Mom and Ebonee were, seen out in public with my largeness. It's natural. I'm sure God has forgiven you."

"I don't understand how I could have done it, the way I've always wanted to see that people are treated equally, the same way I accepted you when we were kids."

She turned her body and smoothed her free hand up and down his rigid arm.

"Analise died years after I saw her on that carousel, but that's the image I carry around. Before I ever told her that I felt ashamed, regretted my actions, and that I loved her." He enfolded Talia's hand, gently held both as though she were a fragile piece of china. "I've dreamt of finding someone else to express my love to. I believe God has brought us together so I'm meant to show you my love. These past few months have given me a peace that makes me think only marriage to a good woman or heaven could be sweeter."

"You must think I'm something I'm not." She stiffened. "I still have deep-seated insecurities, though I know better. I even talked about that with the girls on our walk. I grew up without a dad to call me pretty. I filled that absence in my life with food. It never disappointed and took me away from the hurt."

"Now I'll say how I see you. You're hesitant and don't trust. Keep to yourself when it comes to adult relationships. But you've been freed by the blood of Jesus. You've given yourself to these kids. If you could only see what I'm filling my senses with. I'm positive other adults find you an exotically beautiful, private woman. There's no reason to fear falling short."

"I do hold myself back. I don't want to let anyone down. What if something happens and I get fat again? Then I'd never live up to your expectations."

"I have no expectations. I only want to spend my life with you. So what if you haven't been in the habit of offering yourself. You mistakenly believe exposure of the depths of your heart results in embarrassment or humiliation. You still fear being judged." Cooper cupped her face. His thumbs as light as a breeze caressed her cheeks.

She closed her eyes and allowed her body to calm. He smelled familiar, masculine and alive, so different than she did.

"Listen to your spirit. It could be God's Holy Spirit talking to you. Let me help you get over all of the past that creeps up to bug you. I need your love for my completion. You need my love to fill all those voids. When we're not together, a part of me is missing. That part is you. I need you in my life. Do you love me back, just a little?"

She opened her eyes and covered his hands with hers. Other than pictures of Jesus, Cooper embodied the presence of love. *Oh, Lord, can I tell him how he makes my heart pound to the point of dizziness at times? Is what I feel enough for lasting love?*

Rather than words, she stretched and met his mouth with hers. Oh, the deliciousness, the completeness, the joy of losing herself in another. She had no words. The electric white sparks, the weightlessness, carried her off to somewhere she'd never been.

He pulled back after a time of elation that had taken her to the solar system and beyond.

"All right, Pastor Coop. I'm willing to give the love thing a whirl." *Wednesday night treats turned into Wednesday night meets. Talia and Pastor Coop are in a love loop.*

Chapter 15

THAT KISS SIX WEEKS EARLIER changed Talia's world overnight. Cooper had given her so much attention that the time had flown since then. Spring was definitely the time for blooming love. They'd spent hours talking on the phone at night whenever possible. They spent most of their weekend hours together. Cooper had chosen a particular place for them to sit next to one another during worship on Sundays.

And just like that, it was the last Saturday in April. The youth group partied in the park. Those boys had bottomless stomachs. None of the girls went through the line a second time. Had she given them an eating complex that made them too careful about their food choices? All the cheeseburgers were gone. Chips, salads, and mixed desserts remained.

She swiveled off the picnic table seat with dirty paper products in hand. Cooper swished to her side and took her trash. He leaned in close. "I've got this. I'm ready for you to empty a bag of giant marshmallows into two bowls. Leave the other bowls empty."

Oh boy. What crazy game had he come up with now?

"Hey, everyone." Cooper paused as he called for attention. "Clean up and then we'll take a nose dive after marshmallows. I'll give you five minutes in case you need to take a walk first."

Talia bit back a smile. All these months, he'd never used the word bathroom.

"Two of you, please step forward, hands behind your back." They were so used to girl/boy teams that they lined up accordingly. Cooper continued his instructions. "Please retrieve a giant marshmallow with your mouth from the bowl, carry it to the other table."

Talia groaned with the girls, but held back a grin over the comments.

"Gross."

"Please say we can eat them."

"They'll get stuck up our noses."

"Yuck, snot."

Cooper broke out in a loud guffaw. "Fooled ya. You can eat them. No one wants a goobered up marshmallow dropped into another bowl. If you make it that far without dropping it, Talia will put a fresh marshmallow from the bag into the bowl. If they fall to the ground, please don't step on 'em but pick them up and toss them in the trash. The bowl with the most marshmallows will be the winner. Then they're up for grabs, and you can eat them. Or save them for a party with chocolate and graham crackers."

That comment garnered various eye expressions and head shakes. Whoever said gross was right. Talia tried not to notice all the sticky, slobbery goo on the kids' faces. Saliva and sugar were not a good mix with this bunch.

Once the rollicking was finished and the boys had won, Ransom licked marshmallow off his top lip. "What a foozle game that was."

Sasha shoved him from the side. "I thought foozle was a hairy dust bunny. The kind I avoid, the reason I'll someday have a goldendoodle like Miss Talia. Those dogs are awesome and don't shed."

Burke raised his arms above his head. "Before we get

into the next game Pastor Coop plans to torture us with—"

"Hey." Lydia stepped forward. "We like to eat marshmallows."

"Not squished up our nose. Now, we've planned a game for Miss Talia and Pastor Coop. Take a seat of honor, you two. Face the crowd." Burke waved and the adults were escorted to sit backward at a picnic table bench.

Dustin took over. "We couldn't help but notice how the two of you have become a couple. So we want to know just how much you know about each other."

Janiyah giggled. "Call it junior high counseling before the required pre-marital."

Heat suffused Talia's neck and face. How did she know about that requirement?

Cooper squiggled closer so their shoulders touched. She felt his warm breath near her ear. "Are you ready for this?"

"Better than getting dunked by ice cold water." She slid him a sideways glance. "I'm probably already turning red."

"Get used to it. You're stickin' with me, kid."

The group had clearly planned this. They took turns asking questions as if they'd lined up in order. Well trained.

"Pastor Coop, what is Talia's favorite color?"

He groaned. "Uh, we all know she wears black and white clothes. Her jeep is purple so that's what I'll say."

Talia raised her pointer and drew an invisible slash mark in the air. "Is someone keeping score? Cooper's favorite is orange. That makes us one for one."

"It's no secret Pastor Coop builds birdhouses, what does Talia like to do?"

"Easy. She takes her dog on runs." He jiggled his knees. "Next?"

"Where did you each go to college? Answer for the

other." He indicated for her to go first.

"University of Nebraska, Lincoln."

"Bible College in Omaha."

"Where were you born? Talia, answer for Pastor please."

"Kansas."

All eyes turned to Cooper. "She was born right here in Lincoln."

Lydia wrinkled her nose and swiped black hair off her face. "This is too easy. You know each other well and the score is tied. How about each other's family?"

Cooper squirmed.

Talia tried not to grimace.

They each answered truthfully, she tried to be gracious and only said he had a sister they believed was in heaven. And three brothers.

"Have either of you broken any bones, answer for the other, please."

Cooper made a goofy face and danced his feet in place. Then he held up his hands and shrugged.

"I haven't. But I'm guessing this overgrown kid next to me has. Let me think a moment." She stared off and then jumped to her feet. "Wait. You fell off a skateboard and had your arm in a sling. Collarbone?"

He made a face and nodded.

She chalked the air again.

He stood up and bowed. Facing the youth, he said, "She's now one ahead."

"Favorite foods?"

Cooper made a gagging gesture. "She lives on salads."

"He's a cheeseburgeraholic."

The boys hooted and made extra noises over that answer.

"Miss Talia, describe how you see Pastor Coop."

"He goes to the rescue of those who need it. He's multi-talented, independent yet interactive. Your pastor is moral and practices what he preaches." She gave him a serious glance. "He's never sat down in my home."

"Pastor Coop?"

He shook his head. "For her ears only. You can dock me one."

Her heart beat triple time. She couldn't love him more.

"Okay, we're almost done. Time to tell each other something the other doesn't know. Don't tell about a hidden murder in the family or anything that bad, though."

Talia shifted her body to peer into Cooper's eyes. "At the beginning of the year after we learned the meanings of our names, I was still curious about yours and looked it up for myself. Cooper is one of the oldest names in America, based on a Walter Cooper who settled in Virginia even before the Mayflower landed."

"Wow. You stalker, you." He pecked her on the cheek. Oh boy did that get a reaction of hoots and leg slaps and fist bumps. "I've never admitted that I wasn't quite sure about this youth pastor thing, except that I'm a kid at heart." He paused while the youth shuffled and made gurgling throat noises. "Because of the school year you've given me, though, I believe more than ever that God made every single person worthy of receiving love."

Talia noted soft expressions of wonder on the girls' faces and wide grins on the boys.

He addressed them. "You young people don't need to hear this, but just in case any of you think I'm extra special. I'll confess. No one is perfect, and though we expect other Christians to behave in a certain manner, we should never look up to another person in the place of what God says in the Bible. We all sin. Most of us lie at some point. I admit to feeling jealous about the way my parents gave all their attention to my sister. I felt guilty over that later, and I never felt sufficient self-worth until this woman came into my life again."

Talia wiped a fat tear off her cheek. As she stood, she noticed the same cheek gesture from a couple of the girls.

Cooper snagged a brownie and talked while a few crumbs flew. "Go ahead and have a snack. Miss Talia and I are setting up the next, and last, game."

She opened two bags of balloons while Cooper lined plastic cups upside-down along the edge of a table.

"The object of the game is to blow into a balloon and point it toward the six cups. Hold onto the end while you release the air. As it escapes it's supposed to blow the cups off the table. First one finished with the row wins."

Talia handed out the balloons and Cooper gathered paper cups off the concrete floor of the shelter. Their glances met periodically. She figured her smile was as wide as his. Summer would be bittersweet without the youth meeting every Wednesday. Could she talk Cooper into more dignified dates, maybe go to Omaha a few times for expanded outings? Or sweeter yet, Bible studies on Wednesdays for just the two of them?

He'd told the kids not to build up other Christians in their minds, but he had put her pretty high, feeding into her perfectionistic tendencies. She didn't dare let him down.

She beamed with pride as the young people went into action. Without being asked, they cleaned up trash, covered what remained of cookies and brownies, even emptied drinks onto the grass.

Cooper giant-stepped to her side and almost knocked her over, and then caught her close. "We've done something right with this bunch, wouldn't you say?"

"I'd say you and I make a pretty good team."

Chapter 16

COOPER LED TALIA THROUGH THE park along a paved path, with nervous stomach and calm mind. They meandered close enough that shoulders, arms, or hips occasionally touched. He swung up their hands and pointed to two pairs of scampering squirrels. "They know what spring is all about. And by that Q & A, those kids have shown it's obvious the two of us belong together."

"Don't you just love all of them? They've enriched my life so much that I'll miss them over the summer." She laughed as one pair of squirrels chased each other up and down an oak tree trunk, while the others raced across the ground to another tree. Talia turned to face him, her face alight with joy. "According to Ephesians 2:10, we are God's handiwork, created in Christ Jesus to do good works. God prepared for us to work with these youth together. That just blows me away, to think God had such a plan for you and me eons ago."

He drew her hands to his mouth, catching a faint marshmallow scent, and kissed eight knuckles in a light caress. Then he raised his gaze and their eyes locked in a way that made him weak in the knees. "Miss Talia, who will always be smarter than me and more organized than I am, would you possibly consider sharing this summer with me?" *And a life of summers, but is she ready for me to ask?*

"I think I'd like that. I've learned a lot these past few months. Learning is a two-way street. Those girls have taught me as well, and I know they've learned from us. I hope we all find our bottom-line security, or love and wellbeing, in our Lord Jesus Christ."

"He is our All in All. God proves it over and over again." He tucked a strand of hair behind her ear, reluctant to release it. "I've grown closer to the Lord lately. I'm convinced as never before how much God loves each of us. He doesn't love anyone more than me, and my parents didn't love Analise more than me. God has given me a job to do, along with you, to lead young people in a deeper relationship with Christ and others as well."

"It's a big responsibility. Sometimes I doubt my hang-ups will ever completely go away so I question my ability to help anyone else get over theirs."

"Are we supposed to get over them, or deal by giving them to the Lord when they raise their dirty heads?"

Though he again held onto both her hands, she deflated before his eyes. "The fear is still real at times. I'm so afraid I'll get fat again. I want to be a mother. What if I gain too much and won't be able to lose the pregnancy weight? I never want you or anyone to look at me differently than the way I'm accepted now."

So it wasn't too early to express how he wanted her in his future. He searched her beautiful brown eyes and read her pain.

"You've thought about this. Other than loving the Lord and you, becoming the father of your child would be the greatest honor I can imagine." He ran his thumbs over her soft hands. "Remember, God takes care of tomorrow. Please don't shy away from me." He waited for their gazes to lock. "I tell you now, I'd rather have you with a few extra pounds than watch you become obsessed with what you eat or slip up and get too thin."

They halted their walk at the swings.

He indicated for her to take one, and then he sat beside her, wiggling the chains in a crazy outward motion, bumping her as she settled in the seat.

She kicked off and gained height. "I know these rubber things are safer, but a board seat is so much more comfortable."

He stood back, released, and tried to swing in sync. The woman was fast. She kept pumping higher. Maybe he weighed too much. He leaned back and tried to gain momentum.

She stiffened her arms and stared at the sky. Her glorious black hair grazed the bark chips beneath them. "I love this. At this moment I could be a girl again, without a care in the world."

"Well, I'll be a kid forever. Do you think you could stand having me around for years?"

"You are such a dear, dear man, my Cooper." Talia sat tall and dragged her feet until she slowed to a stop. She didn't quit moving, though, she planted her feet and swayed back and forth, circled in one-eighties. Then side to side as he also stilled. "Shall we make a pact to turn our worries over to Christ and always share what's on our hearts with one another, whether we're feeling like kids or steeped in life issues?"

He pulled the chain of her swing to his side. She shook back her hair, but he reached for the errant lock and rubbed the grapefruit scented strands across his jaw. He searched the depths of her caramel brown eyes. "I wish we could go somewhere only you and I go. A place made for you and me."

She drew his hand away from her hair, smiled in a way that jarred his Adam's apple. "We do. The place we go when you kiss me. No one else goes there."

Aw. What could that ecstatic place be called? Ecstasy? Eden? Rapture?

As much as he wanted to pull her from the swing and cuddle her on his lap, he stood. "At least I can do no wrong in that celestial place, especially considering my bent for perpetual motion." He squeezed her hand. "Would you like to check out those animal rides on springs? I've never sat on one."

She leaped to her feet and ran to a zebra, laughing all the way.

"Ride 'em cowgirl." He chose a leopard, but his knees rose too high for a comfortable experience. "Should have found one of these before I grew up."

"It's not built for my long legs, either. We'd fit on the swinging bridge of that obstacle course, I'm guessing." She pointed.

"Let me escort you, my fair lady." He reached for her hand as she stood and kept her tucked close as they sashayed to the equipment made of composite planking and waterproof rope.

They didn't speak as they maneuvered through tires and climbed with the aid of hand grips to the swinging bridge.

He planted his feet and again drew her to his side. "I believe you recognize that I'm crazy about you. Do you think you could love me for the duration? Since I love you, Talia Ashby, I'd consider it an honor as high as royalty if you would think about becoming my wife."

She pulled back, her hair teasing his palm, and then placed his hands on her waist. She rested her hands on his upper arms. The smile she bestowed on him was as sunny as a daffodil. She cupped his cheek. "I love you back, Cooper. And I believe God created you just for me."

"He created us for one another." He straightened his feet for a firmer stance. His chest expanded as he took a deep breath. "Are you saying you'd like to share a future with me?"

"I can't imagine anyone else loving me the way you do, except God." She groaned and threw back her head. "I can't believe I forgot to tell you something about just how beyond our comprehension He is. Sasha told me that she discovered laminin." She met his gaze. "Have you ever heard of it?"

He shook his head, couldn't hold back a wide grin.

"It has to do with our molecular makeup, a protein in most of our cells and organs. Under the microscope, it's in the shape of a cross."

Wonder spread through Cooper's body like warm lava. Then his forehead creased in thought. "If we have it, even Adam and Eve did. That's mindboggling."

She cupped his face in her hands, smoothed the lines across his brow. The lava flow rose to fever temperature at her touch. He blinked to absorb her words along with the sensations of her fingers.

"I got sidetracked, but God is so amazing I have no words." She traced his mouth with her fingertips, and his whole body quivered as though invisible quicksilver flowed through connecting them as one. She lifted her eyelids, searched deep, drawing him in. "It would be my honor to become Talia Valiant, in due time. I love you with all of my heart."

He couldn't stand not moving any longer. He jumped in the air and fist bumped the heavens. "Yes!!!"

"I believe I know the secret to keep you still, young man. Kiss me, please."

He was more than happy to oblige. And the swaying bridge settled along with his heart.

Enjoy this sneak peek into

MEET

IN THE

Middle

Chapter One

HOW HAD COLIN COME SO low as to stay in his uncle's uninhabitable shack? Especially considering it sat on the edge of this Podunk town, where rumors once abounded about Glen Lovelady's gambling. The bed, such as it was, had him off the grotesque floor. He'd all but covered his head to fight off the chill so, at least to his awareness, no rodents had crept over him during the night.

He fluffed his pillow and smoothed the sleeping bag over the cot. In the gray light of early dawn, he straightened to get out the kinks, rolled and cracked his neck.

The smell hit him. Rotten wood. Mold. Fecund animal droppings. He'd been too tired to breathe last night. Who knew what kind of filth he'd inhaled as he slept? The place looked horrid in the daylight. Unsanitary even for an avid outdoorsman, which he'd never considered himself. He'd have to find a room in town until his next step.

Whatever that might be. What was he even doing here? A desperate move on his part, thinking he could fix up the small house and make a profit so he'd have the means to stay by himself without a job. Just a while longer, at least until the end of summer.

Wouldn't it be something if the rumors about hidden money were true?

He dragged open the door, no easy feat due to the swollen, broken wood panels, and stepped on the rotted porch. A rusty hinge from a nonexistent screen door snagged his flannel shirt. If he attempted to stay, what should he fix first? A sneeze jerked him. No surprise, considering the dust.

He lumbered to his truck, grabbed a reasonably clean napkin from the console, and blew his nose. He stuffed the used napkin in the white sack from last night's drive-through meal purchased halfway between here and Lincoln.

Then he retraced his steps, zipped his pillow inside the sleeping bag, and tucked the bundle behind his truck seat. He sneezed again on his return to the poor excuse for a house, retrieved the cot, where he stored it in the truck bed against the cab.

It may be April, but the onset of spring sparked nary a thought of anything good for Colin. Rather than pay attention to varied greens and the touch of the sun now visible above the horizon, he blinked away from the rising orb. Adam had always laughed at those times the sun's brightness made Colin sneeze. He rolled his shoulders and gazed at the trees lining the Platte River.

And this flat land. It's prime, surrounding Maplewood, his mom's hometown, where its bottom land proved fantastic for producing rich crops.

The distant foghorn of air brakes carried from the highway on the other side of the water, as a semi slowed for the lower speed to go through the village.

Poets no doubt had a heyday penning beautiful words concentrated on fresh mornings such as this, but the glory of the day mocked his severed heart. Let the world welcome spring in all its rebirth glory. The only thing that consumed Colin was loss.

The ecstasy of his own rebirth, thanks to Jesus, just as well belong to some other man. He stretched. "How long, Lord, how long until I want to live as I once did, in tune with Your Spirit?"

It took too much energy to pursue a good mood. Easier to stay low, remaining in a dark frame of mind seemed friendlier at the moment.

Friend. He knew in his head that Adam now spent his time in the presence of Jesus. Yet, rejoicing for his friend's home in heaven escaped Colin's sensibility.

After all, he's the one who deserved the bullet.

The Bible talked about restored joy in the morning. He'd rather stay in the dark and absorb the sound of silence, which had become his latest best friend. But he had no power to stave off a new day. The earth still spun on its axis. Living things continued taking the next breath.

All the while, he wallowed in mourning and fought off horrific nightmares that always ended the same. With him unable to save his best friend.

He stumbled along through the weed-entangled yard. Why had he paid taxes to keep this place all these years? Inherited from his mother, who got it from his bachelor uncle, just to keep it in the Lovelady family?

A wadded ball of dried roots from years of over-grown weeds caught his toe. He staggered, regained his balance, and looked up again. Silly. No one around to see him almost fall on his face. He knelt to untangle his booted foot. Moist soil met his fingertips.

A grunt jerked his head to the right.

He rubbed his eyes in disbelief. He blinked. Focused. Nope. No figment of his imagination. He knew what it was, but he'd only seen the pigs on film.

A pot-bellied pig ambled along the ancient rusted wire of the fence that marked his Uncle Glen's decrepit property, the last acre on this edge of town, bordering a picturesque small farmstead.

Curious, Colin followed the pig's journey as though it was the Pied Piper. Past Uncle Glen's property line and onto the next, which happened to be the first farmstead outside Maplewood.

The pendulous animal snorted again, bobbed its

snout, and a clot of roots topped by dried strands flew to the side.

The act would be funny, if he felt like laughing.

First, they came upon a small shed, bordered by a plot of fallow, unfenced garden. The pig bypassed a row of what looked like maroon tipped flower heads poking through earth like pebbles to greet the sun, and circled toward the only wreck on the place, an old corncrib with the sun glinting through its unpainted ribs on the back of the farmstead.

His steps ground to a halt as he closed in on the leaning building. He stared through the empty center of the peaked structure. The crib. Money. Whoever in the family came up with the rumor that Uncle Glen had buried money near a building? No buildings on his place, except an unsafe, lilting garage.

Details of the old story flew out of nowhere. A notorious gambler, Glen Lovelady never believed in banks. Family lore claimed Uncle Glen had hidden thousands of dollars at the corner of some old building, way back when.

Colin surveyed the surroundings of the neighbor's acreage surrounded by farmland. A garden shed. A detached garage. The corncrib. No barn, outhouse, well house, or machine shed. Such buildings would have existed fifty years ago.

Who paid attention to rumors anyhow?

The reality of buried treasure was way too fanciful for a guy like him to consider. On second thought, he had to pull life together and heal from the incident that stole his normal life.

****

Elena drew in a deep breath and opened the kitchen door off the back stoop. The threshold she'd scarred from an old pair of roller skates welcomed her. She entered the tiny porch into a time past, and straight back to the best memories of her childhood. She gently closed the door as if a slam would disturb the house, and strode into the kitchen.

Her heart raced.

Grandma Merline's hearty welcome didn't resound to immediately fill her with love and acceptance.

Elena pulled herself together. "Stay in the moment."

She stopped in the center of the comfy country kitchen with its red checkered curtains and rooster decor, and closed her eyes.

If the walls could talk, they'd fill her ears with whispered conversations of long ago.

"Listen to the song in your heart." Grandma's voice bounced off the yellow kitchen walls. Did the sweet echo of those sayings linger in all the empty rooms she'd called home for over fifty years?

If so, Elena had plenty more tears to shed.

The farmhouse at the edge of Maplewood, Nebraska, now echoed with emptiness. Yet Grandma's presence couldn't be ignored. It seemed as though she'd just left to tend her garden. Elena imagined the familiar, earthy scent of fresh-picked vegetables, and the faint fragrance of frying chicken. The hint of apples and cinnamon could not be forgotten, or strudel and pumpkin pie.

She sniffed, swiped her left eye.

How would she ever get through this? Grandma had been her only stable influence while growing up. And upon her deathbed, had given Elena the insurmountable task of going through the house and sorting Grandma's belongings. Anything Elena wanted was hers to keep.

Pieces of Grandma's last mumblings wheeled through Elena's thoughts.

"You don't remember your grandfather William. In his own way he was a good man, but he could be hard. He hid something from me that I never laid eyes on. He kept it from me. I know it's still in the house somewhere, and I need you to find it."

What could it be, other than compounding Elena's clean-up task?

Grandma's last phrases were all mixed up. She'd been agitated and adamant. "I know you were happy on the farm as a child. I want you to live there. Find your happy place again."

And the last thing Elena had made out, with a beautiful light on Grandma's face that washed away the years, she'd called out an unfamiliar name. "Glen."

Elena had a new purpose in life, to honor Grandma's memory as well as her last request to find something kept secret. Where should Elena begin to look for some unknown whatever that Grandma claimed to be on the property? How would Elena even know if she found it?

She had triple tasks to accomplish by summer's end. Sort Grandma's belongings. Search for an unknown object. And prove herself worthy of her new at-home job. Adequate internet service in Maplewood enabled her to work from outside Lincoln. The 90-day probation period wasn't really stressful, but if the position didn't work out, would she be happy returning to telemarketing?

After all, she'd been happiest here on Grandma's farm.

Look for the happy during those hours she didn't sit in front of her computer and talk to strangers. Grandma had hinted at something Grandpa had hidden from her. What did that say for the kind of marriage they had?

Along with working so many hours five days a week, she needed to lay out a plan to satisfy

Grandma's request. She must enter each room, each clean room thanks to a couple women from the church, and decide where to begin her search and her sorting.

Not much in the dining room but the antique oak furniture: buffet, hutch, table and chairs. The attic? Grandma's room? Nothing could be undiscovered there, she would have known every nook and cranny of those places.

The hardwood floor squeaked on the way to the stairs, as it always had. She headed up, hand brushing the smooth banister, and welcomed the familiar creak on the third and seventh steps.

The bathroom glowed where sunlight splashed on the porcelain fixtures and checkered black and white floor. The room Grandma had always called Elena's welcomed her as it always had, with its threadbare turquoise chenille spread. Grandma loved her treasured antiques. The dressing table with its splotchy mirror waited for Elena to fill its drawers with her clothing. An open drawer emitted an old scent of floral sachet.

She turned and sighed, still wondering where to begin. Sort or search?

To find anything Grandpa hid, Elena needed to think like a man. Where would a man hide something from his wife, in the basement or an outbuilding? She chuckled. The garden shed belonged to Grandma.

The corncrib was full of boards with space between. That left the garage. She'd check it out, no hurry, but Grandma had parked her car there and stored few things on the hooks and shelves.

How to start then? Prayer. According to Grandma, she'd know the next step by first waiting quietly for the Lord. His prompt would get her going. But how? She'd need her own faith to recognize where to start. She couldn't rely on Grandma's faith.

Pause before you begin. One step at a time. Slow and easy came her first reaction. She giggled at the scritch of the upstairs hall floor. There was no one here to keep quiet for. God sure wouldn't care if the floor or a step made noise.

Elena ambled down the stairs and into the dining room, ran her hand over the corner of the blond table.

Movement drew her gaze beyond the window's lace curtain, past the garden plot. A big dog? A foraging coyote? Too dark in color for a deer.

A second, taller, figure crossed the distance from the property line to the corncrib. Who was poking around the old building? Or was someone shooing off an animal?

She swiveled and headed out of the house. On the way, she ran an eye over Grandma's galoshes, flannel shirt, and heavier jacket. Outside, she lost her footing and slid off the concrete stoop.

Was that really a pot-bellied pig? She straightened. The comical sight drew an immediate lift of her spirits. She'd never seen such a fat hog. But it had to be, since most pigs didn't list so low to the ground, unless it was a very pregnant sow. The oinker must belong to the trespassing man.

Elena strode toward the corncrib, where both pig and man had stopped.

Grandma's voice whispered. "I had a first love that I never forgot." And then she'd said what sounded like, "It was no secret that he didn't trust banks."

Who? Grandpa William, or the unknown Glen she'd mentioned?

"OK, Grandma, get out of my head. I have critters to tend to." Then she laughed. A fat four-legged critter and a lean two-legged one.

The stranger turned as she approached. Shaggy hair the color of rich black coffee. Did those wide-bowed sunglasses hide dark brooding eyes?

"Hey there." His low voice sounded loud in the sudden silence of bird and breeze.

She'd never been jolted by such intensity upon meeting a man for the first time. As she peered at the center of his scruffy beard, his nice lips and pleasant voice drew her closer.

So intent on studying his face, Elena came to a halt at the bump against her leg.

How could the huge, gray spotted pig move so quickly?

The man reached out to prevent her from vaulting over the animal.

At the touch of his hand on her arm, she sucked in a breath. The unexpected, immediate connection threw her. How had he managed to touch her spirit with a mere brush of fingertips?

She lowered her arm and trilled her fingers across the pig's bristly back. "So, what are you and your portly companion doing on my property?"

About the Author

Nebraska country girl LoRee Peery writes fiction that hopefully appeals to adult readers who enjoy stories written from a Christian perspective, focusing on the romance. These include novels and novellas for women and men in the Contemporary, Romance, Historical, Time Travel, and Mystery/Suspense categories. She writes of redeeming grace with a sense of place. Her *Frivolities Series* and the book based on her father's unsolved homicide, *Touches of Time*, are available on Amazon. She is who she is by the grace of God: Christian, country girl, wife, mother, grandmother and great-, sister, friend, and author. Connect with LoRee through these links:

www.loreepeery.com

https://twitter.com/LoreePeery

https://www.facebook.com/LoReePeery

Find her publications at Pelican Book Group:

http://tinyurl.com/kwz9enk

And Amazon:

https://www.amazon.com/LoRee-Peery/e/B004UAGL2W/ref

LoRee's Books:

The Frivolities Series
(White Rose Publishing)
Moselle's Insurance
Rainn on My Parade
Sage and Sweetgrass
Found in the Woods
Dollar Download, Lezlie's Lifeline

Creighton's Hideaway
Paisley's Pattern
Where Hearts Meet

Titles in Pelican Book Group

Christmas Extravaganza:
A Blessed Blue Christmas
Christmas Rescue Route
Christmas 'Couragement
Christmas Trinkets
A Cardinal Christmas
Hiding from Christmas

**Pelican Book Group Devotionals,
including LoRee Peery:**
Red
I Thirst

Coming soon from Pelican Book Group:
Cowboy Just in Time
Future of My Heart
Courting Country

Grace & Victory Press
Touches of Time
Meet in the Middle
Without a Song
Without a Home

Box Set
Life's a Country Song
(Meet in the Middle)

Christmas Stories

Pelican Book Group Extravaganza https://pbgrp.link/2LfF4SR

She's turned her back on her beliefs but recurring visions reveal evidence of true love.

Amazon link **https://tinyurl.com/srh3sql**

Two lonely children met along railroad tracks, where years later they reunite over a lost necklace.

Amazon link: **https://tinyurl.com/yyfh9mn2**
Lonely author meets antiquities owner at Christmas and
matching trinkets open their hearts to love.

Amazon link: **http://tinyurl.com/yccznlb6**

Reunited as adults, can Christmas love conquer the time
between, or create deeper wounds?

Amazon link: **http://tinyurl.com/jd9o5e7**
(Available in audio)

Stranded without wheels, will an independent woman accept aid from a giving, yet needy man?

Amazon link: **http://tinyurl.com/oneqngb**

Murder for hire, a marshal, a boutique owner~ who holds the gift?

Amazon link: **http://tinyurl.com/zwpawsm**

Shana Arnold faces identity theft. Will Creighton Rice help her find her true identity?

Amazon link: **http://tinyurl.com/lpa2l3o**
(Available in audio)

An accusation reunites Lezlie Diamond and Jordan Marshall – will a secret keep them apart?

Pelican link: http://tinyurl.com/ktp3kgn

A woman, a wolf, a man, lost in the woods. Will they find safety?

Amazon link: **http://tinyurl.com/glc2ug4**

Lanae finds a love letter but Sage holds on to the memory of his deceased wife.

Amazon link: **http://tinyurl.com/gu2auy4**

Can Geneva come to terms with younger Rainn's love, still
serve others, and follow her heart?

Amazon link: http://tinyurl.com/p5swlgs

The story that started LoRee Peery's publication career, the first
in the *Frivolities Series*:

Can they forgive one another, and accept that true love never
dies if it's ordained?

Amazon link: **http://tinyurl.com/k642v7m**

Are obedience and trust in God enough to keep Deena and Simon from chasing memories?

Amazon link: **http://tinyurl.com/o3sn5qk**

Grace & Victory Press

Touches of Time
is based on LoRee Peery's father's unsolved homicide.

A graphic artist embarks on a journey to discover who killed her grandfather. She wants a whodunit answer for her unborn child. Can she accept what she does, or does not, find on her quest, including the Investigator's deception?

Amazon link: **http://tinyurl.com/jofktnj**
Barnes & Noble: **http://tinyurl.com/zmg858g**

Can a country stay mend the broken hearts of a recent widow
and a disillusioned songwriter?

Amazon link: **https://tinyurl.com/y3tbn4mt**

Can a cowboy without a ranch come to terms with his amnesiac,
homeless old flame?

Amazon link: **https://tinyurl.com/v9yburh**

She finds a love letter, he acts on a rumor, and a pig provides
resolution.

Amazon link **https://tinyurl.com/y4rlwufo**

Box set

Amazon link https://tinyurl.com/yyr99ssj

Find out more about this author at **www.loreepeery.com**